where

we belong

Alabama Summer Series, Book Four

J. DANIELS

This book is dedicated to Kellie Richardson.
Of course.

where

we belong

Alabama Summer Series, Book Four

mia

I F SOMEONE WOULD'VE told me ten, fifteen years ago that not only would I eventually like Benjamin Kelly, my greatest tormentor, but that I would fall completely in love with him and marry the guy . . . well, I'm not sure what I would've said. Ten, fifteen years ago I probably would've directed whoever was spouting that nonsense to Tessa and let her handle them.

Even as a preteen, she would've had a very colorful response.

But me? I think I'd have stood there, disbelieving, probably a bit disgusted, but maybe, *maybe* the tiniest, concealed part of me would've smiled a little at the idea of him liking me, falling completely in love with me, marrying *me*.

I like to imagine there was always some part of my soul that belonged to Ben. Something undeniable tethering us together. An imperceptible energy, like the force behind a gust of wind.

It's always been there.

It's what brought me back to Ruxton, Alabama three years ago. It's what put Ben in the bar that night. And it's what made falling in love with him so incredibly simple.

All those years I hated him seem like a lifetime ago. One which never even belonged to me. I don't remember those emotions. I don't remember the pain and hurt he caused me.

The detestation I felt.

I look at my husband and the only thing I see is love. The only thing I feel is love . . .

Love.

Love.

Love.

My mind loves Ben. My heart loves Ben. My body loves Ben. He's the warmth in my blood. The roar of my pulse.

Give me a hundred years with Benjamin Kelly, and I'd still beg for more.

Lately though? With two boys who have mastered the skill of interrupting Mommy and Daddy the second we put our hands on each other, I'm not making unrealistic demands. I'm asking for one hour.

Give me one hour alone with Benjamin Kelly.

I'll beg for that.

At this point, I'll beg for five minutes.

mia

TURN THE baby monitor on and set it on the nightstand by the bed.

The blue light flickers, picking up every restless noise Chase makes as he tosses around in his crib. I can picture him rubbing his sweet, dimpled little face into his blanket. His purple octopus tucked under his arm. He always sleeps with that. It's his dragon.

My two boys, land and sea.

I gaze at Ben's side of the bed as I strip off my shorts and sleeveless blouse, slipping one of his Ruxton Police Academy T-shirts over my head. The comforter is creaseless. Undisturbed. I plop down on the bed with a heavy sigh and hug his pillow to my chest.

One more night.

I miss him, and not just when I'm alone like this after I put the boys to bed. I miss Ben getting home when I'm making dinner. I miss him being up with us for a few hours, spending time with the boys and helping with them. I miss the way we'd come together after getting them off to sleep, two pounding hearts colliding in a tangle of limbs and hurried breaths in the hallway, dragging each other to the bedroom, tearing at clothes, sometimes making it to the bed, sometimes not. The floor. Up against the wall. Me, bent over and holding onto anything I could grab. We'd stay quiet, the soft slapping of our bodies barely audible above our heavy breathing and desperate moans. He'd tell me to come, *fucking come, Mia*, and I would, writhing against him while he gave me his release and every ounce of love he could pour out of himself. We'd tumble onto the bed, still clutching at each other, his mouth pressed to my skin and his fingers between my legs, pushing back inside of me.

I'd fall asleep wrapped in his arms, feeling so small and so safe, my heart so full of him.

I love nights with Ben, but right now, and for the past two months, my nights have been his mornings.

While I'm giving baths and going through bedtime rituals, he's leaving for work. And because I'm giving baths and going through bedtime rituals, he's not pressing me up against any walls or tearing off my clothes. He's not biting or tasting my skin. He's not getting off. I'm not getting off.

In fact, that hasn't been happening much at all lately.

Two boys tearing through this house, exploring and getting into anything and everything, with one now unfortunately out of the nap stage has made it nearly impossible to get any alone time with Ben. Throw in two months of night shift and I can't remember the last time we were both awake and grasping at each other without immediately getting interrupted.

It's like kids have this built-in radar. This sixth sense that goes off whenever Daddy grabs Mommy's boob. Their timing is honestly quite impressive. They never miss a beat.

It wasn't so bad before. I would laugh it off and grab Ben's face, kissing his scowl and promising to work him later. We'd get the kids to sleep and then he'd grab me, or I'd grab him, or we'd both just be grabbing and tasting and not caring who was doing what as long as it was happening. And it was always happening.

Now? Nobody's grabbing or tasting anything. We don't have our nights. When Ben's home, I'm with the boys and he's getting his much needed sleep. Everything is ass backwards.

But, there is a light at the end of this miserable tunnel. After this last shift, we can go back to our routine of stolen kisses and heated seconds before one or two little faces catch us. And when they do, not if, it won't be detrimental. I'm sure I'll still be kissing a scowl and muffling words I don't want repeated, but we'll have those sweet hours between evening and dawn where there's nothing and no one between us.

No interruptions. Just two pounding hearts, feverish touches, and that quiet climb toward rapture, followed by the sweet, blissful fall.

Sliding beneath the cool sheets, I exchange Ben's pillow for my own and nuzzle my nose against it, inhaling him, letting his scent soak into my lungs. That distinct Ben smell that carries so many memories with it.

Ones of us together, that night after the bar. My first hit.

God, I've been addicted to him ever since.

I flip onto my back and grab my phone off the night stand. I brush my hair out of my face and type a quick text.

Me: Missing you. XO

Holding the phone above me, I snap a selfie, blowing him a kiss, and attach it to the message, sending it. I scroll to Tessa's number and hit dial.

She answers after two rings.

"I don't know about you, but I am so ready to hop off the 'nobody's getting laid' train."

"What?" I chuckle, shaking my head at my best friend and stretching out my limbs. "You're getting laid. What are you talking about?"

"Not the way I want to be!" She sighs. "I mean, okay, don't get me wrong. I don't mind waking Luke up for a nooner, but I miss when we would just fuck all night like we were trying to repopulate the earth after an apocalypse."

"Well, be grateful you're at least able to sneak it in during the day. Even with Chase taking a nap I can't catch a break. Nolan can't be unsupervised."

It's bad timing all around. Both of my boys have been in on this together from the beginning.

When this dreaded night shift started, Nolan was in school for half of the day. As long as Chase went down for his nap, I could have some alone time with Ben.

Seems like a flawless plan, right?

Wrong.

Chase wouldn't nap until Nolan came home from school. I should've known, my sweet boy needs constant noise to pass out. The non-stop chatter of his big brother seems to do the trick. This was also around the same time Chase became extra clingy, refusing to allow me even a moment of privacy to use the bathroom. So, when I thought I could sit him in his high-chair with a few toys and sneak into my bedroom for a quickie, he would scream, and scream, and scream, like someone was actually hurting him.

I felt terrible. I scolded myself for being the worst mother on earth. How could I put my own needs before his?

Now that Nolan's off for the summer and home twenty-four hours a day? Chase naps anytime I want him to and doesn't even flinch if I need to use the bathroom.

Their plan has been flawless from day one.

Tessa yawns, breaking up the soft noise of the T.V. in the background. "Just put on a movie for him or something. Or tell him to go play in his room. This is what iPads are for."

"Tessa, you know how curious Nolan is. He hears a door shutting anywhere in this house and he comes investigating. And I swear to God, he knows when I'm naked and barges in at that exact moment. He's just like Ben."

"Those Kelly boys," she laughs. "Tits men for life."

I roll my eyes. "It's in their blood."

"Speaking of tits, I wanna go out and get a new bikini for the wedding. Mine are all faded from my parent's pool."

The wedding, Reed and Beth's. We're all heading down to Sparrow's Island next week for the ceremony. Beth really wanted to get married on the beach, and her sweet aunt and uncle are sparing no expense. From the pictures I've seen online, the beach itself is beautiful. White sands and crystal blue water. Tessa and I are in the wedding, along with Riley, Reed's sister, Ben, Luke, CJ, and the boys. We're all staying in villas right on the beach with spectacular views of the ocean.

I can't wait to get away for a few days. After the past two months, I feel like we all need it.

"You know, when you say you want to get a new bikini for the wedding, it sounds like you're actually going to wear it during the ceremony," I tell her, smiling. "You are planning on wearing the dress Beth picked out for us, right? They've already been paid for."

Tessa gasps. "Oh, my God. Can you imagine Ben if you wore a bikini during the ceremony? He would gouge out every pair of eyes belonging to men within a fifty mile radius. You should absolutely do it."

"What?" I giggle, shifting on the mattress a bit.

Is she crazy? He would do more than gouge out their eyes.

"What about Luke? What would he do if you wore one and he saw you walking down the aisle half naked?"

"Luke?" Tessa pauses, thinking silently for a minute.

"Mm. He'd probably drag me down to the sand and fuck me in front of my parents. Like a savage."

"Oh, that's nice. I'm sure Ben wouldn't mind watching his sister being taken."

My phone beeps with an incoming text. I hold it above me.

> Ben: *Goddamn, angel. This is the worst possible time for my dick to be hard.*

My cheeks burn. *Oh, is it?*

I place the phone back to my ear, catching the tail-end of Tessa's amusing reaction. "Hey, I gotta go. Let me know when you want to run out and I'll go with you."

"Cool. I'll ask Beth too. One more night of this sexless hell."

I laugh. "Yeah. See ya."

I end the call and run my tongue along my bottom lip as I type out my response.

> Me: *So telling you how wet my fingers are isn't something you should know right now?*

> Me: *Oops . . .*

My phone starts to ring, startling me and wiping the smirk off my face. Running my free hand over my racing heart, I answer the call in my most nonchalant voice.

"Hello?"

"Mia," Ben growls.

The hairs on my neck stand up.

Shit. Is he pissed?

"H-Hi, babe. I wasn't really . . ."

"How many fingers are you using?"

His question squeezes the air from my lungs, or his

demand, rather, because that's what it sounds like. An order, spoken by the only man I've ever gotten off with, for, from. You name it. Ben *is* and always will be the only man, and right now, he isn't asking how I'm touching myself. He's making sure I'm doing it.

While he's at work.

Hot holy fuck.

I wet my lips again as I slide my hand down my body and into my panties, over my sensitive flesh and through my slick heat. "One," I softly reply, my voice shaking, my fingers soaked and trembling.

His heavy breathing fills my ear. "You pretending it's me, angel?"

"Yes."

"You forget how thick I am?"

I close my eyes, moaning. "Jesus, Ben. Are you by yourself?"

"Do you really think I'd be getting my wife off over the phone with Luke's nosey ass sitting next to me? I told him to take a walk."

A smile pulls at my mouth.

Seriously stupid question on my part. Of course Ben wouldn't be speaking to me like this if anyone was in hearing distance. He doesn't share my pleasure. The times that he has taken me while we've been out in public have been rare occurrences, and ones I usually beg for.

"You can be quick," I'll tell him. *"And I can be quiet."*

He'll debate both of my suggestions with believable resistance, but once my top comes off he forgets how to argue.

"Baby." Ben's voice sends a shiver up my spine. "How many fingers?"

"Three." My breath hitches as I stretch myself. Wetness

trickles onto my palm. "So wet," I whisper.

"Fuck, I wish I was there. Touching you. Sliding inside of you. Is that what you want? You want me to fuck you, Mia?"

"Yes," I gasp.

"I wouldn't be slow, baby. God, I couldn't. Not tonight. I need you . . . on my cock. That sweet, wet pussy gripping me." His breath starts coming out in sharp pants. "Spread your legs. I want them wide, angel. Come on."

My hips burn as I bend my knees and pull my legs up. "They are. They're so wide it hurts."

"Good. Now fuck yourself like I would. Fast, baby. I want to hear it. Wanna hear how wet you are."

Moaning, I think about Ben next to me, hovering over me, his wild gray eyes locked between my legs while I pump my fingers in and out. In and out. Faster. My thumb brushing over my clit, rubbing it like he does.

I twist my wrist. A soft squelching noise tickles the air.

"Do you hear me?" I ask, my heart racing and my breathing sharp. *"Ben . . ."*

"Angel," he growls, his voice vibrating through my body. I swear, it gets me wetter.

"Keep going. You're making such a mess for me, aren't you?"

"Yes, it's . . . I'm dripping. On my hand. Oh, God, Ben."

"Fuck."

He sounds desperate. Just as turned on as I am.

I picture him stroking his cock while he watches me. He's throbbing, the head red and swollen. Dripping. *Oh, God, he's dripping too.* He uses two hands, gripping his balls while rubbing his shaft against my thigh.

"Wanna feel you squeezing my cock, baby. Milking me. Come on. Take those fingers like you take my dick. Come all over them."

OhGodOhGodOhGod.

"Ben," I whisper, arching my back. My legs shaking as that delicious heat spreads up my spine. "C-Coming. I'm coming."

I drop the phone, squeezing my breast through my shirt, moaning into the silence of my bedroom and then falling weightless against the sheets, my body limp and warm. Sated.

Satisfied, but only as satisfied as I can be when he's not here losing control with me.

"Hey." I press the phone to my ear and squeeze my legs together. My face feels hot. "I miss you."

I listen to his slow, heavy breathing.

"Me too, Mia. This kills me. You know that, right? This separation I feel. Not being with you the way I fucking need to be. I feel like I'm going crazy."

A tinge of guilt grips at my chest. "Me too."

"And here you are, taking care of our boys, sending me sweet pictures and getting off thinking about my cock."

I smile, rolling over and facing his side of the bed. "Your perfect cock. Nine inches of perfection."

He laughs, a deep rumbling sound. "I love you."

"I love you. One more night."

"Yeah." He sighs.

I can picture him relaxing, his thick shoulders dropping down and his head falling back. The tension leaving his body.

"One more night," he echoes. "I'm warning you, Mia. Once I get you alone again, I'm fucking you all over that house. All night. I don't want to sleep."

"Okay," I giggle. "But we'll have to sleep some. Just a couple hours."

"You can sleep. I'll just keep fucking you."

"Ben," I laugh harder, covering my mouth.

"Christ, I love that sound. Close your eyes and pretend I'm with you."

"Okay." I close my eyes, listening to his breath in my ear, hearing it grow tenser and tenser with each passing second. "Luke is coming back, isn't he?"

"Fucker. I told him to stay gone until I called him. I'm still sporting a semi."

"Aw, babe. Do you know what I would do if I was there?"

"Mia," his voice is a warning.

"I'd drop to my knees and lick . . ."

The line goes dead.

Oh, I really, really hope he gets me for that.

I close my eyes, smiling and welcoming sleep.

"I'll be waiting, Officer Kelly."

ben

CUTTING OFF THE engine to my truck, I take the keys out of the ignition and step down, shutting the door and walking up the driveway toward the house.

At 8:15 a.m., the sky is blooming with bright colors, the sun already warming the air.

I rub at my neck, squinting a bit to avoid the harsh morning light.

Fucking night shift. I couldn't be happier about switching back to days. Going two months without spending any real time with my family has taken its toll. It's been tough on everyone. The boys don't understand why I'm not around as much. You can't really explain it to Chase yet. Not even two years old, he's still too young to get why I have to work at all. Nolan is used to me leaving him during the day. I've been doing it for the past six years, but in his mind, the bad guys should be sleeping when the rest of us are. He thinks the entire world shuts down at night.

I wish it did. I miss my sons. And Mia, fuck, I miss her so badly I fucking ache. I'm not ashamed to admit my dependency on her. That woman keeps me breathing, and for the past two months, she's done more for our family than she probably realizes.

I can't wait to worship every perfect inch of her.

Stepping up onto the porch, I hear Nolan's animated voice

somewhere in the house. Chase squeals, probably laughing at his brother. I unlock the door and step inside, moving toward the noise in the kitchen.

I stand in the entryway, going unnoticed, leaning against the wall and watching my family.

Nolan is seated at the table, eating pancakes and drawing in his sketch pad. Chase is next to him in his high chair, reaching with both hands for the plate of pancakes on the table and out of his reach. He kicks his feet and whines.

"Shh, Chasey," Nolan says, keeping his head down and concentrating on his paper. "You're messing me up."

"Hold on, baby. I'm just getting your milk."

That sweet, velvety voice draws my attention across the room. Desire throbs low in my groin. Just hearing her and I'm fucking ready.

I look at Mia.

She's standing at the bar with her back to me, pouring some milk into a cup for Chase. Her dark hair is falling halfway down her back, messy from sleep. She's wearing one of my shirts by the looks of it. It hangs loose on her body, the sleeves touching her elbows and the hem covering her ass, revealing long, tanned legs and bare feet.

Christ, I'm a lucky bastard. Still can't believe that perfection is mine.

"Daddy!" Nolan jumps from his seat at the table and lunges for me, clinging to my leg. Chase starts chanting, "Da-DaDa" over and over like he does when he spots me, and Mia spins around, smiling and biting at her lip, looking like she's got a million dirty thoughts running through her head as her eyes run up and down the length of me.

"Angel."

She winks, then turns back to put the milk away, her hips

swaying as she walks to the fridge.

Remembering my boys are in the room, one still stuck to my leg, I will my cock to ignore my wife and her slamming fucking body, which is damn near impossible, and grab Nolan, picking him up, smiling when he runs his finger down my nose. I do the same to him and he giggles.

"Hey, buddy. You being good?"

"Yeah. I made my bed all by myself today. Chasey can't do that yet."

Chuckling under my breath, I carry Nolan over to the table and sit next to Chase, smiling at my other boy. I grab his sticky fist and kiss it.

"Little man. You hungry?"

Chase looks down at the plate of pancakes again and reaches for them, making all kinds of grunting noises, his face turning a deep shade of red and his brown eyes round.

"He's had a whole pancake already, Daddy. Mommy said he's going to eat us outta the house. I don't want that. I like it here."

Mia laughs behind me.

Smiling, I grab the fork and feed Chase a bite. "He's a growing boy. You ate like this when you were his age. How do you think you got those big muscles?"

"I'm gonna be as big as you. Look." Nolan flexes his arms, the sleeves of his T-shirt coming up to reveal his tiny biceps. "See? And I'm gonna have tattoos like you too. Just on this arm. A big dragon." He runs his hand over his right shoulder and down to his elbow.

Mia walks up to the table, setting Chase's cup on the highchair. "And what about your girlfriend's name? Aren't you going to get that on you somewhere too?"

Nolan sighs, his shoulders sagging as he drops his head.

He tugs at the buttons on my uniform. "I don't have a girl-friend. I told you that. I can't find one I like." He looks up at me. "But I will, Daddy. I'm going to have her name just like you have. The first girl I get."

Smiling, my chest swelling with pride, I glance up at Mia, then look back at my son. "You got plenty of time, Nolan. Don't worry about getting any girl's name tattooed on you until you know you're marrying her, okay?"

He slides off my lap. "First girl I like, I'm marrying," he mumbles, climbing back into his seat and resuming his drawing. Another castle, by the looks of it.

Jesus. I hope that isn't the case. How many fucking mistakes did I make before I wised up and went after what was in front of me most of my life? Angie being the biggest slip-up, though I'll never regret what resulted from our one drunken night together. I wouldn't have Nolan if it wasn't for that massive error in judgement.

It's a strange thing, hating someone but living for what they gave you. Having Nolan changed my life. I'd never take it back. That doesn't change or lessen my feelings toward his mother. In my opinion, she doesn't deserve to live. I don't care how harsh that is. I'll die hating that bitch. She nearly took my entire world away from me.

Mia bumps her hip against my arm. "He's just like you," she whispers, her eyes falling over my shoulder. "He loves with every part of him."

I grab Mia's waist and pull her into my lap, wrapping my arms around her and tucking her as close to my body as I can get her. I bury my face into her neck and breathe.

Just. Fucking. Breathe.

I close my eyes, moaning when she runs her fingers along my scalp.

"You tired, babe?"

"Mm." I nod a bit, rubbing her back.

Truth is, I'm fucking exhausted. The muscles in my back and shoulders feel tight. My head is pounding, courtesy of the last call we got, and the woman who yelled in my ear for twenty fucking minutes about her ex stealing money out of her safe and threatening to hit her. Luke handled him while I tried to calm her down. Didn't work. She was still screaming to no one in particular when we pulled away from the house.

I just want to sleep. I need it after the night I've had, but fuck, I want this more.

Turns out, Mia plans on deciding for me.

She stands and tugs my arm, getting me out of the chair. "Nolan, watch your brother for a minute. If he drops his cup, pick it up for him, okay? I'll be right back."

Nolan nods, leaning on the table and coloring in his drawing.

I'm led down the hallway and pulled into our bedroom. Mia walks around the bed to the window, closing the blinds and drawing the curtains.

"Long night?" she asks, going to the bed. She pulls down the comforter and sheet on my side.

I step further into the room. "Yeah," I answer, rubbing at my face. "Fuck, though, I don't want to sleep, Mia. I don't need it."

Sleep or her? My choice is incredibly simple.

She looks up at me, those big brown eyes going soft. "Come here," she whispers.

I start unbuttoning my shirt as I round the bed to get to her.

"Don't. Let me do it."

She brushes my hands away and takes over, starting at

my collar and working her way down to my belt. She looks up at me and untucks my shirt, then sucks on her fat bottom lip as she pushes it off of my shoulders.

I start breathing heavy, my need for her sparking in my gut like a live wire, my hands clenching and unclenching at my sides.

She grabs the hem of my white T-shirt and lifts it up my ribs. I take over and reach behind me, pulling it off and tossing it onto the floor. Then her hands are on me, rubbing my abs, my chest, wrapping around my biceps and squeezing.

I watch her stare at me, the way Mia has always stared at my body. Her eyes wide and absorbing, taking in every inch of me, lingering on the ink covering my arm, her name above my hip, and the muscles cut into my skin, looking like she's never seen anything more beautiful before. It makes me feel conceited as fuck. I'm not an arrogant guy. I never gave a shit about what women thought of my body, even though I've always busted my ass staying in shape.

But Mia? Fuck, yeah, I want to be beautiful for her. I want her to always look at me like this.

She presses her lips to my chest.

My blood runs warm, warmer when her hands tug at my belt.

"I missed you," she says, coming up on her toes and kissing my jaw. "So much, babe."

I grab her face, guiding her mouth to mine, kissing her as my pants hit the floor. "Baby," I moan, my breath hitching when she squeezes my hips, so close to my throbbing cock that's pressing against her stomach.

She pushes against my chest. "On the bed."

Fuck, yes. Finally.

I sit on the edge, ready to sink back onto the mattress for

the ride of my life when she climbs behind me and wraps her arms around my front.

She sighs, kissing my neck and shoulder where the tiny scar mars my skin from when I was shot. Her hands spread across my chest. "The boys and I are going to the store in a bit so you'll have some quiet. Try and sleep as much as you can."

I look down at my cock tenting my boxers. "Angel, you just got me real fucking hard, and you expect me to sleep?"

"How?" she giggles. "From undressing you?"

I shake my head. "Living, Mia. Just you being here, loving me, fucking walking around this house wearing my ring and being mine . . . Jesus, yeah, I'm tired, baby, but I'll sleep when I'm dead. Not now. Not when I can be with you."

She presses her front to my back, squeezing me tighter and moving her lips to my ear. "You, Benjamin Kelly, can be so sweet when you want to be."

I grunt. "I'm sweet to you all the time."

"Sometimes you're just dirty."

I turn my head. Our eyes lock. "You want dirty now?"

She purses her lips, fighting a smile. "No."

"No?"

"I want you to get some rest."

Leaning in, she seals our lips together, sucking on my tongue when I force it into her mouth, moaning a little and pressing her heavy tits against my back.

"You're going to need it, Ben," she whispers. "I'm going to ride you so fucking hard, you're not gonna be able to walk tomorrow. And not just your cock, babe. I'm riding this sweet fuck-me mouth too."

Jesus FUCK.

Groaning, I palm my dick, feeling like I could come right now just from the filth spilling past those perfect fucking lips.

"But only if you sleep."

Kissing me one last time, she slips off the bed and scurries to the door.

What?

"Damn it, Mia," I growl, falling back onto the bed, turning my head and watching her lean against the door frame and blow me a kiss. My body goes lax, sinking into the mattress. *Fuck, it feels good to lay down.* "I don't need sleep," I tell her, yawning at the end of my protest, rubbing at my face again and rolling over. "Not tired, angel."

I am so fucking tired.

My eyes close. I reach blindly for the pillow Mia used last night and press it against my nose.

Berries and cream. Fucking heaven right here.

"I love you."

Mia's soft voice and the latch of the door closing is the last thing I hear before sleep easily pulls me under.

I RUB A towel over my head and down my arms, absorbing the water from my skin as I stand in the bathroom.

I've slept for close to ten hours. I feel reenergized and ready to fuck my wife into next week.

God, she has no idea what she's in for, baiting me like that. Telling me she was going to ride my cock and my face before slipping out of reach. She'll be lucky if I let her control any of this. Maybe after I've taken her bent over the bed and pounded her into the mattress I'll let her grind that sweet, wet pussy against my face while she laps at my cock.

Maybe.

I just want to take and take and take tonight, fuck Mia until my body burns with exhaustion. Until there's no space between us, no separation.

Nothing. Just us.

The boys are still awake. I can hear them tramping down the hallway as I pull on a pair of loose shorts and a T-shirt. I open the bedroom door and step out, scooping up both of my sons and hauling them over my shoulder, growling at them while they squeal and squirm in my arms.

"Daddy!"

"DaDaDa!"

Mia moves toward us, shaking her head through a smile, those tight jeans on her hips looking like a damn second skin. Her shirt dipping low in the front.

Christ.

She motions at Chase's bedroom door. "Bed time. Come on, Daddy."

I give her a look. *"Daddy? You calling me that tonight?"*

She smiles, her cheeks tinting with color. She wets her lips. *"Maybe."*

Moving with purpose, ready to get these boys down and get on my woman, I follow Mia into Chase's bedroom and let Nolan slide down to the floor so he can go play with his train set we keep in here.

He runs to it, banging the pieces together on the tracks, immediately making the noise his brother needs to fall asleep.

I shift Chase in my arms and kiss his head. I look up at Mia. "You want me to put him down?"

Chase reaches for her. "MaMaMa."

Stepping closer, Mia rubs his back. "Sorry," she whispers, looking up at me with soft eyes. "I think he's gotten a little attached to me since you've been gone. I'll do it tonight." She takes him from my arms and carries him to the crib, sitting down in the chair beside it and rocking him against her chest.

I move to the wall and lean against it, arms crossed, just watching her as Nolan continues to play, making all kinds of noise no one should be able to fall asleep hearing, but Chase is like that. The louder the better for him.

He had colic when he was younger and wouldn't sleep for anything. He was so miserable. We tried the normal stuff, but even Nolan banging around in here wouldn't put him down. On the brink of losing my mind, I grabbed the vacuum and ran it next to his crib for thirty seconds.

Put him right out.

After a few minutes, Mia stands and moves to the crib. Chase is out cold, already snoring a little.

"Nolan, come on. Bed time."

Nolan leaves his trains and dashes out of the room. I follow behind. As I'm entering his bedroom, he grabs his stuffed dragon off the windowsill and carries him to the bed.

"What's he doing over there?" I ask, tucking Nolan in and sitting on the edge beside him.

He usually carries that thing around with him everywhere.

Nolan squeezes the dragon to his chest. "Keeping watch for bad guys. You weren't home last night." He shrugs a little, turning on his side and facing me, his big gray eyes blinking heavily. "Mommy says I'm the man of the house when you aren't here. My dragon was helping me protect us."

Grinning, feeling so much pride for my son and loving how honest he has always been about everything, sparing nobody's feelings in the process, I bend down and kiss his head. "Love you, buddy," I whisper, watching him slip the ear of the dragon into his mouth, his eyes falling closed and his deep, even breathing settling him.

I step out into the hallway and pull the door shut.

Looking up, I spot Mia standing by our bedroom door,

her top unbuttoned, hanging open and revealing most of her bare tits, stripped of her jeans already and standing in nothing else except the tiniest pair of white panties, looking like no more than a few pieces of dental floss strung together.

"Baby."

My voice sounds hoarse, need filling every fiber of my body as I move toward her, my eyes raking over her tiny frame, from her toes to those big eyes holding onto me, up and down again until I can't fucking see her 'cause she's pressing against me, crawling up my body, her legs wrapping around my waist and her fingers gripping my hair.

"Bedroom," she whispers, sucking and biting my neck. "Hurry, Ben."

I get us through the doorway, and that's about as far as I make it before she's sliding down my body and hitting the ground with her knees, tugging my shorts down to my mid-thigh and gasping when my cock springs free.

No boxers.

"Mia," I moan, my head rolling back as she licks the under-side of my shaft, cupping my balls in her hand and squeezing gently. I close my eyes, fisting some of her hair. *"Fuck."*

"You taste so good." She sucks at the head, making little mewling noises in the back of her throat like she's fucking starved for me, tonguing my balls and pumping my shaft. "You're so beautiful, Ben. Even this."

I look down with heavy eyes, staring at my wife. My angel, my sweet fucking angel on her knees worshipping my cock, sucking me into the back of her throat and bobbing with vigor, her small hands squeezing my thighs, tensing every time she gags.

Her lips wet. Her eyes watering.

That familiar pull drags through my groin and pricks low

in my spine. The threat of release.

I don't want to come yet, not before Mia. Not before I do everything I've been dying to do to her since I stepped inside the house ten hours ago.

Moaning around my shaft, she sucks at me, hard and hungry.

I close my eyes.

Pace this shit, Kelly. Remember all the filthy, perverted acts you wanted to do and fucking do them before . . .

My breath hitches when Mia bites down a little, dragging her teeth, giving me that tiny bit of pain she knows drives me fucking wild.

Jesus, FUCK.

Moving back, I slide my cock out of her mouth and grab her arms, tugging her to her feet. We switch positions, me dropping down to my knees and her standing above me, posed to be adored, the way it always should be with us.

Planting my hands on her waist, I spin her around until she's facing the wall.

"Lean forward. Stick your ass out, baby."

With a gentle hand, I guide her, pushing against the small of her back until her hands are flat on the wall and her head is bowed, her legs trembling as she spreads her feet.

"Oh God," she whimpers, looking down at me over her shoulder as I spread her ass with my hands, moaning and leaning further into the wall when I kiss her pussy from behind, the gentlest press of my lips to her heated flesh.

I'm ready to devour her, my mouth watering at the very idea of Mia's taste coating my tongue when a loud, screeching cry sounding like something out of a nightmare comes echoing into the bedroom, sending Mia and I both ramrod straight.

"Chase! Oh, my God." Mia slides her thong back into place and starts frantically buttoning up her shirt as she darts out of the room.

I look down at the state I'm in—my dick out, hard as a fucking rock and pointing straight up at me, tenting my shirt. My shorts down around my thighs, and my brain, fuck, that has to be around here on the floor somewhere. Pretty damn sure Mia sucked it out of my cock when she was going at me minutes ago.

That woman. Fuck me.

Hearing Chase's worrying cries still going on in the other room, I scramble to my feet and pull up my shorts, my heart racing as I cross the hall and enter his bedroom.

Mia is clutching him to her, kissing his cheek and trying to settle him. "I think he had a night terror. He's shaking, Ben, and his little heart is pounding so fast."

I rub his back and brush his dark hair off his forehead.

He's still crying, and I can see how worked up he is. I can hear it in his labored breathing.

What the hell do kids this little dream about that scares them like this? Clowns? Fucking deranged cartoon animals?

"Let me take him," I tell her, pulling him into my arms and against my chest, dropping my head next to his.

Chase fists my shirt and rubs his face against mine, his crying growing a little softer.

"Mommy?"

Lifting my head, I spot Nolan in the doorway.

He rubs at his eye, peering at us both and looking too exhausted to stand.

"Hey, come here." Mia goes to him, kneeling down to cup his face. "You okay?"

"Is Chasey going to sleep with you?"

Mia looks back at me expectantly, a smile pulling at her mouth.

She knows why she's smiling. I sure as shit know why

she's smiling.

My boys are cock-blocking me. Again, because this definitely isn't the first time. I swear they plan this shit out at dinner.

I look down at Chase, his eyes wide with alarm and his little body still trembling with confused fear. No fucking way is he passing out any time soon, not looking like this. And Nolan, hell, if he knows Chase is lying in bed with us, he'll fight his way into that room swinging every damn sword he owns.

Jerking my head, I walk toward the two of them. "Come on. But we're sleeping, Nolan. We aren't playing in there."

Nobody is playing in there. Not anymore.

"Yesss," he whispers, sounding a bit excited.

Mia rubs my back as we head into our bedroom.

She and Nolan climb on the bed first after she tugs on a tiny pair of pajama shorts and a night shirt.

I lay Chase next to Nolan and sink down beside him, keeping him close to me as I roll on my side to face everyone.

Everyone. All three pairs of eyes open and fixated on me.

"Nolan," I warn, and immediately he shuts his eyes and rolls over, putting his back to me. I wrap my arm around Chase, trying to soothe him as Mia watches me from over the top of Nolan's head.

Her eyes full of love and warmth, sucking me in just a little bit deeper.

"*Sorry,*" she mouths, smiling a bit.

I shrug.

"*I love you.*"

Heat blooms in the center of my chest.

I stare back at her, suddenly not caring at all that our night got interrupted, only feeling content and fucking whole being this close to Mia and our boys.

"Love you, angel," I mouth back, hearing the buzz of my phone on the night stand behind me, a call I'm going to ignore no matter who the fuck it is.

It can wait. This, right here, nothing is more important than this.

Everything else can wait.

mia

"**H**OLY SHHH . . ."

"Tessa!"

Pulling the boys against me, wrapping an arm around each of their heads and doing my best to cover both pairs of innocent ears, I glare at the burgundy dressing room door my foul-mouthed best friend stands behind, glaring even harder when the door cracks open and a green eye peers at me.

Do you mind?

Tessa opens the door a bit wider and looks between the two boys, not appearing all too apologetic. "My bad. But it's not like they haven't heard it before."

"Doesn't matter. Just wait until you and Luke have a kid and they start repeating everything you say."

I lower my hands, allowing the boys to move around in front of me again as I remain seated on the cushioned bench.

Her eyes widen a bit. She seems to tense up. "Let me get changed," she murmurs.

The door shuts. I hear the soft rustling of clothes and the clink of a metal hanger.

I immediately regret bringing up the kids topic. Tessa always gets quiet when I mention her and Luke starting a family, and if I pry she shuts down even more, changing the conversation or just leaving the room entirely. I think the whole thing worries her. She lost Luke three years ago because she didn't think he wanted kids. Even though they're solid now and married, I think a part of her still fears something tearing them apart.

After several minutes, her dressing room door opens and she steps out, holding the lingerie she went in to try on—a plum-colored, lace-trim babydoll.

She sits down next to me, crossing her one leg over the other and clutching the garment.

"I'm buying this. My boobs look enormous in it."

I let out an exhaustive breath, looking from Nolan, who is giggling and covering his mouth, to Tessa, who is also giggling, poking him in the stomach.

I'd scold her for that if Ben wasn't so keen on talking about my breasts when Nolan is still in earshot.

He's heard every slang term in the English vocabulary. He's even shared some with his friends at school.

We've been called in to speak with the teacher twice now. Ben couldn't act more proud sitting in on those meetings, puffing his chest out, looking at his son like he's raising some sort of breast connoisseur.

I'm usually the one doing all the apologizing and swearing up and down certain words will never be repeated.

Tessa nudges me with her elbow, leaning in to whisper. "So, are you as deliciously sore as I am? Luke's been on me like flies on shit."

Crossing my arms below my chest, I lean back against the wall, sulking. "No. We haven't done it at all."

God, I miss sex with Ben. Delicious, mind-numbing, earth-shattering sex with Ben.

"What? They were off for two days. What have you two been doing?"

I motion at Chase and Nolan as they follow each other around the small dressing room area, Chase trying to catch his big brother with his arms outstretched, and Nolan, laughing and letting him get real close before he darts away.

"Oh," Tessa mumbles, leaning back next to me, both of us watching the boys. "Well, what about after they go to bed? That's your usual playtime, isn't it?"

"Not lately. Chase keeps waking up within a couple minutes of us putting him down, and Nolan always hears him. Then he's up and wanting to sleep with us too. Ben wants me to ignore it, but I can't. I've tried. I hate hearing Chase cry like that. And poor Nolan. Ben yelled at him last night 'cause he was sick of getting interrupted and Nolan stuck his little fingers underneath our bedroom door and cried until we let him in."

"Jesus."

"Yeah, I've tried praying about it. That's not working either. I don't know what to do. If Ben doesn't take me soon I think he might go crazy. I caught him researching the damages of sex withdrawal yesterday while the boys were eating lunch."

Tessa chuckles. "Oh, my God. I'm so glad I know this information. I'm going to tease the hell out of him now."

"Please don't," I groan. "I'm sure he's already getting it from Luke."

"Exactly. We can both play off his misery."

I glare at her.

She smiles, her one dimple caving in and her shoulders lifting in tiny jerks as she continues to laugh.

"I know what you should do," she says after a minute, looking serious now. "Get him while he's at work."

My mouth falls open. "What? How? I have the boys."

"Not if I take them for you. Drop them off at my house and find out from Luke where he's at. Surprise him. How many times have we talked about doing it in the back of a cop car? One of us needs to make that happen ASAP."

Biting the inside of my cheek while I contemplate this suggestion, I feel my body relax against the wall. My muscles going slack. "Mm."

How many times *have* we talked about this? More times than I can count. It's a major fantasy of mine, but one I never have the opportunity to act on because of the boys. Just the sight of Ben in his uniform is enough to make my legs shake. Pairing that with us crammed into the back of his car, him pinning me down or me grinding in his lap, his pants undone just enough to reveal his cock, the harsh chill of his handcuffs pressing into my skin, biting my flesh, the smell of sex and sweat growing thick around us and lingering there after we're done, reminding him every time he gets in what we did and how it felt . . . Yeah, that's definitely something I've thought about more than once.

"Mm mmm." Tessa wiggles her brows. "Just let me know when and we'll make it happen."

Warmth spreads across my face.

Now? Is that too short notice?

Sighing, Tessa leans forward, braces her elbows on her knees and stares at the door next to the one she was occupying minutes ago. "Beth, you did want us here with you today so you could get our opinions, right? We can't really do that unless you show us what you're wearing."

A soft, throaty grunt sounds from behind the door.

I smile.

Sweet Beth. She's a little anxious about her wedding night with Reed. I get it. She wants him speechless at the sight of her, in her wedding dress and out of it.

Oh La La Boutique has just the thing for that.

Her door opens slightly. She peeks her head out, looking hesitant, her dark brows pulled together and her lips pinched into a tight white line. "Okay . . . ready?"

I look over at the boys, making sure they're occupied with each other and not in her line of sight. Nodding, I motion for her to show us.

Releasing a tense breath, Beth steps back and pulls the door open, standing in her dressing room to stay concealed.

She's wearing a white embroidered corset with delicate lace trim, the material tight across her body, showing ample cleavage and her cute little curves, a matching garter and white stockings on her legs.

"Wow." My eyes widen. *Reed is going to lose his mind.*

Beth runs her hand across her stomach, still looking unsure. "Honestly, do you think he'll like it? I've never worn anything like this before."

"Seriously? Will he like it?" Tessa laughs. She presses her hand to her chest. "*I* like it. I would marry you if I knew that was on underneath your dress. You're going to give him a heart attack in that thing."

Beth covers her mouth, her cheeks flushing. "Yeah? I just . . ." She lowers her hand. "I want him to want me so bad, like how I want him. You know?"

I smile at her, feeling so happy for both of them.

Especially Reed. He deserves this kind of love.

"Well, I don't think that's going to be a problem. I say buy it," I tell her, standing and moving to the boys when Chase starts whining. I pick him up and bounce him in my arms.

"Me too," Tessa adds.

"Okay. With the stockings, or . . ."

"With," Tessa and I answer simultaneously.

"All right," she giggles. "Cool. I need to hurry and get

changed so I can get back to the bar."

Her dressing room door closes.

Tessa stands from the bench and moves across the dressing area. "What about you?" she asks.

"What about me?"

"Hello." She hooks a thumb over her shoulder toward the doorway leading out into the store. "Go pick out something and try it on."

Chase squirms in my arms, forcing me to switch him to my other hip. I shake my head. "They're getting restless. We need to get going. And when will I even have the chance to wear it for Ben? Next year?"

I'm certain Tessa plans on wearing her hot little number when we all go away for the wedding, most likely even before that. She has plenty of opportunities to put on something sexy and let Luke slowly work his way peeling it off.

Mine and Ben's situation is different.

Putting on lingerie for him at home will only amp up his frustration when he can't keep his hands on me for longer than a minute, and the boys are staying with us in the villa for the wedding. We won't be having any alone time together during that little romantic rendezvous.

Maybe when they both graduate and head off to college we'll get some privacy? My luck, Oh La La won't even be around anymore.

Tessa's mouth stretches into a knowing smile. "Oh, I don't know. Maybe you can wear something extra spicy when you surprise him in the back of his cop car." She tilts her head to see behind me. "Hey, Nolan. Wanna go get some ice cream?"

Anxiousness settles inside my gut.

Yes, the cop car. We'll definitely be alone there.

Nolan scrambles out from behind my legs and punches

his little fist into the air. "Oh, yeah! I want cookie dough!"

"What are you doing?" I ask her.

Tessa pries Chase from my arms, then digs into her back pocket and pulls out her keys. "Here." She presses them into my palm. "Give me your set. I'll take the boys to Baskin Robbins. You can meet us there when you're done shopping for my horny brother."

I would cringe at that comment if I wasn't used to Tessa's inappropriate mouth.

My shoulders sag as I reach for my keys, handing them over at the same time as asking, "Really?"

She takes them. "Really. I'd say go find out where Ben is when you're done but I have a massive stack of transcripts I need to get through today. Let's shoot for tomorrow instead."

I lunge at her, careful of Chase, and wrap my arms around her neck. "Thank you," I whisper, feeling incredibly grateful.

I can see the light at the end of this sexless tunnel, and it's shining on Ben's massive cock.

Beth emerges from her dressing room carrying her wedding day surprise for Reed. She smiles at us. "We going?"

I give the boys each a quick kiss, grinning so big my cheeks hurt.

"You two are. Mommy's doing a little shopping."

THE WHITE LACE panty and matching bra set I'm standing in is doing wonders for my curves, and my tan.

My skin looks even more sun kissed than it does after I've spent a full day at the pool with the boys. My breasts are pushed up high on my chest, doubling my normal cleavage size.

I'm certain Ben will have no problem with this . . . development. I suddenly look like I'm still breastfeeding.

Sheesh. He was a maniac that first year. I'm not sure who was more starved for my chest. Chase or Ben.

I run my finger over the ruffles along my hip, loving the overall delicate look and feel to this set. Still unbelievably sexy, but soft.

Understated. I like that.

Spinning in front of the mirror, I glance over my shoulder and blush a little at the sight of my bare ass. I stand on my toes and pop my hip to watch it jiggle.

Mm. Maybe I won't make Ben wait until tomorrow . . .

Blowing out a quick breath, I reach for my shorts on the small bench and dig out my phone.

I've sent my fair share of dirty pictures to Ben. He always responds with something equally vulgar, words I'll read over and over until I'm trembling against my hand, dropping my phone and panting his name. The moment he sees me, he'll pull up whatever it is I sent him and we'll both look at it while he beats into me from behind.

Maybe this is cruel, since I know we won't have that time together tonight. I'll get him hard and leave him even more frustrated, but we'll have tomorrow. He doesn't know it, but I'm going to make up for every interrupted opportunity tomorrow.

Every. Single. One.

Pushing my hair off my shoulders, I lean forward a little and snap an up-close shot of my breasts, my hand squeezing one of them. I attach the photo to a message.

Me: Yours.

After setting my phone down, I unclasp the bra and slide it off my shoulders. I step out of the panties and grab the other ensemble I brought back to try on, a black sheer babydoll.

The silk slides over my skin, clinging to my hips and brushing against the top of my thighs.

I run my hands over my stomach as I stare at myself in the full length mirror.

I like this one too. Again, massive boob appeal. My legs look never ending. Plus, I love how soft it is against my skin.

I palm my phone again, studying the screen and waiting for Ben's reply.

It never comes.

Maybe he's busy?

After tossing my phone back onto my pile of clothes, I glance at the tag, then do a quick calculation of the two outfits together while tapping my finger on my lip.

When was the credit card paid? Two, three weeks ago? I should be able to charge both, right?

"Mia?"

My head snaps to the right. I stare at the closed door concealing me, the bottom stopping at the floor. I'm completely hidden.

He's here.

My stomach flips wildly.

"Ben?" I whisper. Twisting the knob, I pull the door open an inch.

His dark blue uniform is the first thing I see, stretching wondrously across his broad chest and shoulders, then his neck, his Adam's apple bobbing thickly.

Why that makes me wet, I have no idea.

My gaze moves over the sharp angle of his jaw, dusted in light stubble, and as I lift my head and our eyes lock, the last thing I see is the hunger sparking there, his irises practically vibrating with need before he pushes the door open and pins me against the mirror.

"The boys," he growls, slamming the door shut, ducking his head and nipping at my jaw, his large hands grabbing my hips and squeezing. His chest heaving, pressing hurriedly against mine, pushing me higher and higher up the mirror until my feet come off the floor.

My head rolls back with a gasp. "Tessa has them. They went to get ice cream."

"*Jesus*. That picture, Mia. I've never driven so fast in my fucking life."

He roughly kisses me, burning my jaw with his stubble but I hardly care.

I slide my tongue into his mouth and grip his biceps, digging my nails into his hard muscle.

We kiss and kiss and kiss, until my head is spinning, until I can't see or feel or taste anything besides Ben.

Only Ben.

"I need you. Fucking need this. I can't breathe," he says.

I moan and fall limp into his arms.

He's here. It still isn't sinking in that Ben's touching me, that his hands are roaming down my back and pulling up the material of my lingerie, grabbing my ass, the hard line of his cock pressing against my stomach while he licks and sucks my neck, while he hitches my legs around his waist and drops his hand between us, working at his belt.

He's *here*. He should be at work. He should be out patrolling with Luke. And instead he's initiating public sex . . .

This never happens.

"Whoa, wait." I push against his chest, just enough to make him lean back and look at me. "You want to do this now? Here? Someone could hear us."

"Baby," he rasps, staring into my eyes. "Yeah. Here. Right fucking now. You can be quiet. And no one can see shit from out there. I couldn't see you before you opened the door."

"What about Luke?"

"What the fuck about him? He's in the car, where his ass needs to stay until I'm done."

"But . . ."

But? Why am I protesting this? SHUP UP, MIA!

"Damn it, Mia," Ben growls. "If I don't get inside you, my balls are going to fall off. I'm dying here."

Grinning, threading my fingers through his short hair and tilting my head up to kiss his jaw, I tighten the muscles in my legs and draw him closer.

"What are you waiting for then? Get that monster out."

His entire body shakes, a shudder rolling through him. "God, I fucking love you."

I smile wider, pressing my lips against his mouth and sucking at his lip.

Fumbling between us while supporting my weight, Ben frees his cock, leaving his pants up, his shirt on, everything in place except his belt, the button on his slacks, and the zipper.

Like my fantasy, I think, squirming and clawing at him, begging for it, my voice quiet and urgent.

He cups my pussy and slips two fingers inside.

"Ben," I whimper as he stretches me. "Please . . . please, I need it."

"You need what?"

"Your cock."

He grins that beautiful, heart-stopping grin, the one that altered the course of my life that night in the bar three years ago. The only one he ever gives me.

"Yeah, you do," he growls, slipping his fingers out of me and holding the base of his cock, leaning forward and pushing the tip inside. "You fucking need it. Need my cock fucking this sweet pussy, don't you, angel?"

I close my eyes, feeling him, feeling nothing but him.

"Yes," I whisper.

He slides in so slowly, barely moving.

A little more . . . my legs shake. A little more . . .

"Hey! That guy's stealing stuff! Hey, stop him!"

My eyes snap open.

Ben freezes, barely inside of me, every muscle in his body tensing while his hot breath bathes my face, bursting across my skin in sharp pants.

"Hey!" Someone else yells. "Hey, wasn't there a cop in here? I saw him! Where did he go? Hey, help! This guy is stealing stuff! Help!"

"Fuck!" Ben yells, his voice echoing off the walls as he puts me on my feet and tucks his erection away.

Growling, his entire body radiating an anger unlike anything I've ever seen before, the veins in his forehead threatening to burst and his teeth clenched so tight he's hissing his breaths now, he grabs my face and kisses me hard before wrenching the door open and storming out of the dressing area.

"Mother fuck!"

Grabbing my shirt, I cover myself with it and follow behind, staying shielded by the wall and looking out into the store.

"Richardson! You piece of shit! Come here!" Ben rounds on a big bald guy hunched over a table and tucking handfuls of women's panties into the neck of his shirt.

Gross.

"You are fucking dead!"

I stare, wide-eyed as Ben pulls the guy up, nearly lifting him off the ground before he slams him against the wall and cuffs him.

I've never witnessed Ben arresting anyone before, or really doing any type of police work.

Sweet mercy.

This is foreplay right here. The best kind of foreplay.

The authority in his voice, the way he's showing his power over this creep, cuffing him with one hand while keeping him pinned to the wall.

I might have to start doing ride-alongs.

"The fuck, Kelly?" The guy yells, struggling against Ben's hold and craning his neck to see behind him. "What the fuck are you doing in a women's lingerie store?"

Ben leans in closer. "What the fuck are you doing stealing panties, you sick fuck?"

Grinning, the guy limply shrugs. "You found my fetish. No shame in my game."

"Ew. Get him out of here."

"Yeah, that's sick. The cop is crazy hot though. I mean . . . *damn.*"

"Seriously. I might steal something while he's in here."

I smile at the small group of women standing by the registers. I'm used to the general public gawking at Ben.

I gawk too. Allll the time.

Ben yanks the guy back, pulling him off the wall and moving toward the entrance. "Didn't you see the squad car outside? Are you that fucking stupid you'll try and rob a place with a cop parked in front of it?"

"Figured you were in the donut shop on the corner."

My mouth falls open.

So stereotypical.

"Yeah? Well, fuck you. I only go there on Fridays."

Shaking my head, I press my fingers to my lips and smile against them.

Ben gets to the door, looking back at me over his shoulder. "Buy them both," he yells, that dimpled grin on his face, and I know he means the outfit I'm wearing and the glimpse of the one he got in the text.

The small group of women all jerk their heads in my direction, gaping at me.

I look from them proudly back to Ben, waving and smiling big, watching as he hauls the creepy panty-thief out of the store. My eyes lowering and lingering on his firm ass.

And I gawk. I mean . . . *damn*.

ben

"**W**HAT THE HELL? No bachelor party? How can you not have a bachelor party? It's tradition, man."

I swallow my mouthful of beer as CJ returns to the table, carrying a long neck for himself and handing one off to Luke. After taking a swig, CJ spins the vacant chair next to me around and sits in it, leaning his elbows on the high back and staring expectantly across the table.

"It's your last night of freedom," he adds, persistent with his argument. "You're just going to pass that up?"

Reed shrugs off the question, sliding his hand around the bottle in front of him. "What the fuck do I care about having a bachelor party? The only woman I want grinding in my lap is that sexy as hell waitress over there."

Leaning back in his chair, Reed strains his neck and looks across the room at Beth as she carries two plates out from the kitchen and walks them over to a booth along the wall.

"Goddamn," he groans. "I get to marry that."

As if hearing or sensing the attention she's getting, Beth looks up at that exact moment and smiles at Reed.

"*Jesus,*" he mutters.

A laugh rumbles in my chest.

Christ, he's fucking whipped like the rest of us. Never thought I'd see the day.

CJ sets his beer down on the table. He looks between Luke and myself. "Come on. Sin City? Nobody else thinks we should've gone to Vegas or something?"

"To gamble?" I ask, grinning, already knowing the answer. He's not pushing a bachelor party to hit up any casinos. "That's probably not a good place for you. No offense, man, but you suck at poker. How many times have I cleaned you out?"

"Is that relevant? They have live sex shows there. Girl on girl. Who the hell said anything about gambling?"

"You know you can't participate in those, right?"

He cocks his head. "Do you own the fucking Vegas hand-book? How do you know? They could ask for a volunteer."

"Right."

Shaking my head, I dig my phone out of my back pocket when it starts to vibrate with a call. Seeing the unknown number again, I hit ignore and toss it onto the table in front of me.

Fuck. I'm going to have to deal with this shit soon. She keeps fucking calling.

CJ turns his attention on Luke. "What about you? Wouldn't you have gone to something like that?"

"Have you met my wife? Mouthy redhead?" Luke lifts his bottle for a drink, his eyes widening a bit. "I like my balls where they are."

"Pussies," CJ grumbles. "All three of you."

"Man, what-the-fuck-ever. You're just looking for an easy opportunity to get your dick wet," Luke says. "Go fucking nuts at the wedding. Women are always horny as shit at those."

Reed jerks forward in his seat. "You better not go fucking nuts at the wedding."

CJ frowns. "Why not?"

"Why? You're paired up with my sister, that's fucking why. Keep your dick in your pants and stay the hell away from her."

"How am I supposed to do that if I'm paired up with her, dumbass?"

"You know what I mean," Reed growls. "Don't make me regret asking you to be a part of this. You walk her down the aisle, you dance with her for that one required song, and that's it. After that, you don't know her."

"What if she wants to dance with me more than once? I'm just supposed to tell her no? That's fucked up."

"She won't."

"Really?" CJ cocks an eyebrow, looking arrogant. "Hate to break it to you, man, but I'm a phenomenal dancer. Took classes and shit when I was a kid. Slow, fast, I can do it all. Trust me. She'll want another dance. They always do. And I'm not a dick. I'm going to dance with her if she asks me."

Reed narrows his eyes.

"Especially if she's hot," CJ adds, smiling and nodding slowly. "Is she?"

Gritting his teeth, Reed glares across the table, looking almost as murderous as he did that night in my kitchen when CJ was hitting on Beth in front of him.

They've become close since then. It's one of the reasons why Reed asked him to be in the wedding. Another was Beth. She's good friends with CJ now too. Doesn't matter though. A sister is a sister. My best friend married mine and I still pound on Luke if he says anything even remotely sexual about Tessa in my presence.

Or if he thinks it.

I lean forward and slap CJ across the back of the head. "Shut the fuck up before he beats on you."

He jerks his head in my direction, rubbing at his scalp. "You know we're about the same size, right, Kelly?"

"About." I grin. "You think you can take me?"

"I took Jacobs."

"Fucker, we all took Jacobs. He was such a little bitch," Luke laughs, setting his bottle down and smiling big, no doubt remembering that in-service training day and the ass-kicking he gave Jacobs in the ring.

Out of all of us, Luke despised him the most. Luckily, when Luke surrendered that detective position and got his ass back to Ruxton to fix shit with my sister, Jacobs took the job and left, leaving CJ without a partner.

CJ doesn't seem to mind his absence. No one does. Jacobs was a shit cop and a douchebag human being.

"I kinda miss that asshole," Luke adds dryly, scratching the back of his buzzed head. "Remember how pissed he'd get when his lunch would go missing from the break room? His wife made the best chicken salad."

"That was you?" CJ's brow lifts to his hairline. He snorts, his hand falling heavy on the table. "Man, do you know how many times I was stuck listening to him bitch in the car about that? He was already annoying as shit."

"Why did you all hate him?" Reed asks, looking between us.

"'Cause he was a dick. Plain and fucking simple."

I nod in agreement with CJ, taking another swig of my beer.

Luke rubs at his jaw, his eyes losing focus as if he's remembering something. "Caught him checking out Tessa's ass one time a few years ago."

I slowly sit forward. *The fuck?* "What?"

What the hell? I didn't know about this.

He lifts his gaze. "Yeah. It was right after she and I first met and she stopped by the precinct to visit you. But I think she was really just there wearing those damn cut-offs trying to bait me."

I glare at him.

"With conversation," he quickly adds, blinking away.

"Conversation?" Reed breathes a laugh, looking skeptically at Luke. "Yeah, right. I know what cut-offs you're talking about. I watched her hack up a pair of old jeans to make them. She wasn't there to talk, man."

I cut Reed a look.

I'm not sure what's pissing me off more, the fact that he probably watched my sister try those damn ass-hugging shorts on since the two of them are so fucking close, or the fact that he's right.

My sister sure as hell wasn't there to talk, to me or Luke.

I remember her stopping in that day. I remember wondering what the hell she was doing stopping in, since she never came by the precinct before. After giving me no more than two words, greeting me with a 'sup bro?', she immediately narrowed in on Luke and the two of them disappeared together.

That fucker came back inside twenty minutes later wearing the biggest, shit-eating grin on his face and begging me for Tessa's number, telling me she was sorry she couldn't stay and chat.

Yeah. I'm sure she was devastated.

Reed's face drops all trace of humor when he absorbs my reaction. Clearing his throat, he lifts his beer and chugs half of it.

I look around the table.

I should line these idiots up and knock them out one at a time. Then I should go find Jacobs and bury him.

After mentioning it was Luke eating his sandwiches all those years. Be fucking awesome seeing him react to that news.

"Hey, guys." Beth walks up to the table and places her

hand on Reed's shoulder, smiling at each of us before looking down at him. "Hey you."

"Sweetheart," he replies, reaching for her. "Come here."

She shakes her head. "Can't. My shift isn't over."

"I'll handle that. Where's Danny? I'll threaten to start calling him Dad again." Reed starts to get up.

"Reed," she laughs, pushing against his arm until he lowers back into his seat. She bends down and drops her head next to his.

They share a moment, whispering with each other, Reed cupping her face and kissing her, looking more than ready to marry his girl.

It's good to see. I'm happy for them. Really fucking happy for Reed.

Doesn't mean I won't give him shit about it while I can. What are friends for?

"You ready to marry this idiot?" I ask, my voice lifting as I stand and slip my phone away.

Reed narrows his eyes. I ignore it, smiling at Beth.

"It's not too late to back out."

She slides into Reed's lap and wraps her arms around him, holding him possessively.

"I was born ready," she declares, tilting her chin up, owning those words and saying them loud enough I'm sure a few tables around us hear her.

An emotion passes over Reed's face, something I know I feel a thousand times a day when I think about Mia. He looks relieved, like he's finally able to take a breath after going so long without it, his eyes going soft before he slowly closes them.

Dropping his head, he buries his face in Beth's neck and pins her against him.

I take that as my cue, as do the other guys, who stand,

leaving their beers on the table and reaching for their wallets.

I want to get home to Mia anyway. It's been three hours since I left her in that dressing room looking like straight-up sin, begging and needing what I was offering her. I'm dying to see her.

Hold her.

Taste her.

Touch her.

Fuck her.

My groin throbs.

Fuck. Get home before you get hard.

After tossing out some cash to cover a tip, I walk out of McGill's Pub with CJ and Luke, the two of them talking shit about Jacobs as I glance at the phone vibrating in my hand.

I hit ignore for the second time tonight.

"I PAID FOR my mistakes, Ben. I know what I did was unforgivable . . . but he's my son. I want to see him. I have every right to see him. You can't keep Nolan from me. And ignoring my calls? Really? Answer your damn phone. This isn't . . ."

"Ben?"

Hearing the voice behind me, I cut off my second listen of Angie's voicemail and lower my hand, clutching my phone and keeping my back to Mia as I try and work this bullshit out in my head.

Truth is, I don't want to work it out. I knew this day would come, and I'm not ready for it. I'll never be ready for it.

I feel Mia's tits press against my back. Her hands wrap around my waist.

"Babe?"

"Angie's out. She wants to see Nolan."

Mia tenses, the muscles in her arms going stiff. "What?" she whispers. Her hands slowly leave my body. "Why is she out already? I thought she was supposed to get four years?"

"Good behavior," I mumble, spinning around.

I toss my phone on the bed behind Mia and rub at my face, my breath blowing hot against my palms.

"Good fucking behavior. It doesn't matter that she could've killed Nolan. That she could've taken my son from me. No, she's been playing nice with the guards and doing a real good job cleaning toilets. Let's let her out early. She fucking deserves it."

I start pacing the room.

That night three years ago when I got the call from Rollins plays back in my mind. It stings like a fresh wound, pitting deep in my chest. I'll never forget it. I'll never forget how scared I was for Nolan and the unforgiving rage I felt for his mother, seeing her in the back of that squad car crying and begging for compassion, spouting her excuses to me, trying to justify shit. I didn't want to hear her fucked up reasoning for driving drunk and high with my son in the car—blaming me. Saying I gave up on us.

She could've killed Nolan, and she wanted my understanding? My empathy?

Fuck her. I will never forgive that bitch. She thinks she paid for her mistakes? She thinks I owe her time with my son? I don't owe her shit.

"What does this mean? You have full custody. Do you have to let her see him?"

I grip the base of my neck. "I don't know. Technically, when one parent has full custody, the other has visitation. You work it out together. If you can't, you go to court. That's what happened when Nolan was born. Angie got full custody."

What a fucking joke that was. She should've never had custody of Nolan. Never did anything with him. Never paid him any attention when he was in her care. She acted uninterested in being his mother half the time, and the other half she spent keeping my time with him as limited as possible.

"Yeah," Mia whispers. "But this is different, Ben. She put Nolan in danger. How can they let her have any time with him?"

"Because she's the mom. They could grant her visitation based solely on that. Maybe supervised. Maybe not. I don't know, Mia. The only cases I know about where one parent doesn't get any visitation with their kid at all is if there's been a history of sexual or physical abuse. Something that extreme. I don't know if Angie's mistake would prevent her from getting to see Nolan. It fucking should, but if we go to court a judge could favor against me. I don't want to risk that. There is no way in hell I'll ever leave her alone with him. Court ordered or not, that cunt isn't getting any privileges."

She's not taking my son from me. From Mia. I don't care what I have to do. I won't let that happen.

This is his home. His family. She doesn't deserve to know him.

The boys scamper into the bedroom, chasing after each other and laughing.

It stops my pacing.

I look up at Mia and see the worry in her eyes, the tears building there and threatening to fall as she keeps her gaze lowered.

She doesn't even react to the commotion in front of her.

Fuck. I'm making this all about me. I'm forgetting how much this affects her too.

Chase squeals, following a giggling Nolan out of the room

and back down the hallway. Their laughter fades. I watch as Mia turns and picks my phone up off the bed and walks it over. She presses it into my hand.

"Mia."

"You need to call her," she says quietly, blinking and sending a tear down her face. "You have to, Ben. Work this out somehow. I'm afraid if you don't she'll just stop over here. I don't want her confusing Nolan like that. It's not fair to him."

I grit my teeth.

I know Mia's right. Angie can and will stop over here if I don't deal with this. She'll eventually stop calling and seek me out another way. I need to handle this shit now, but my only real concern at the moment is standing right in front of me.

I lift Mia's chin, forcing her to look at me.

"What are you thinking, angel? Talk to me."

She shakes her head slightly. Her breath bursts against my wrist.

"They're selfish."

"What are?"

"My thoughts. What I'm thinking. What if Nolan chooses her over me? What if he wants her to be his mommy again? I know he has that right. Angie's always had that claim to Nolan, but he's my son, Ben." Her chin wobbles. Another tear wets her cheek. "He's *my son*."

Her soft voice breaks, and it kills me. Seeing this woman, my salvation and the best thing to happen to Nolan worry that she'll lose him to someone who doesn't deserve any right to him. It fucking kills me.

I hold her cheek. "You are more of a mother to Nolan than she ever was. Everyone sees that. Nolan sees it. He would never choose her over you."

"You don't know that," she softly replies, pulling back

out of my grip and moving away.

"Baby."

She looks at the phone in my hand while wiping at her face, trying to compose herself as fresh tears brim her eyes. "Call her. Set something up and take Nolan over there."

I move toward her. "We'll do it together."

"No." She shakes her head, halting me.

My eyes go wide.

No?

"I don't think I can," she says, holding my gaze but looking like she's struggling to give me this honesty. Looking like she's scared to acknowledge it.

Mia isn't the type of person to put her needs before anyone else's. She's always thinking about me and the boys first, herself last. I know this is killing her. She doesn't want to recognize her fear, but she is, and she's looking like she hates herself for feeling it.

"Just do it, Ben, okay? Please? Don't ask me to go."

I swallow thickly as Mia leaves the room.

Collapsing onto the bed, I stare at the phone in my hand, pull up my missed calls, and hit dial, fueled by one thing driving me to do this. The only reason I'll ever have.

My wife.

"Ben?"

My free hand makes a fist at the sound of Angie's voice.

"Listen, and listen good, 'cause I'm only saying this once. I'll bring Nolan over to see you, but it's going to be on my terms. When, for how long, what the fuck you two talk about. All of it. Every time he sees you will be on my terms, and that's only if he *wants* to see you. I'm not forcing my son to spend time with someone who gave up every right to him three years ago. You didn't just make a mistake, Angie. And you sure as fuck don't have any claim to Nolan anymore. Don't feed me that bullshit again. You hear me?"

"Y-Yeah," she stutters. "I hear you. But Ben . . ."

"But nothing. You think you paid for this? You think spending three years in jail erases what you did? It doesn't. You could've killed him. I don't give a shit how long you spent locked up. I don't care if you never see my son again. And if I'm being perfectly fucking honest, if this was up to me and I wasn't worried about making the woman I love happy, you wouldn't be spending any time with Nolan. Judge or no judge, I will always do what's right by my kid. I will always protect him. And keeping him far away from you is the best thing for him."

There's a short pause, then Angie's meek voice finally comes through the phone. "I'm sorry. I am. I know I fucked up. I . . ."

"I'll bring him over when I get off tomorrow. Where are you staying?"

She sniffles. "My sister's house. 85 Lakely Circle. By the mall."

"Fine. Don't expect this to be some sort of reunion. We're staying for a couple minutes and then I'm taking him home to his family. If he's not comfortable, or if he wants to leave before that, we're gone. Do you understand?"

"Yes."

I end the call.

Staying hunched over, my elbows resting on my knees, I close my eyes and fill my lungs with air, releasing it slowly. I repeat this until the tightness in my shoulders subsides.

Mia doesn't think she can handle this tomorrow. I won't force her to go, but I know my son. I know how much he adores Mia. How much he has since they first met. Their connection was immediate. Undeniable, like the one I have to her. She was always meant to be his mother. And she's worried she's going to lose him to a woman he never had a relationship with. To a woman who never deserved to know him.

I roll my neck, opening my eyes and staring at my phone.

We need some time together. Fuck the past two months and this bullshit. Mia shouldn't be worrying about anything.

I pull up my contacts and dial Tessa. It rings once.

"Your wife already called me," she answers, confirming what I had been thinking. "I can't believe that bitch is out of jail already. You call her back?"

I pinch the bridge of my nose. "Yeah. I'm taking Nolan over there tomorrow. I just want to get this over with."

"I don't blame you. But if you ask me, she doesn't deserve to see him. She doesn't deserve anything besides being a fuck doll for the scariest bitch in D block."

I almost laugh. If I wasn't consumed by this, by Nolan's possible reaction to seeing Angie tomorrow and Mia's worry I'm taking on as my own, I might've.

"Listen, I'm not calling to talk about Angie. I need a favor."

"What? Oh, and I have something for you. It's not important or anything."

Standing from the bed, I move to the doorway and peer into the hall, making sure I'm alone. "What is it?"

"It's just something I think you'll want to have," she says teasingly. "A little memento. I'll give it to you next time I see you."

I don't have time to play Tessa's games. Mia could come down the hall at any second.

"Fine. Look, I need to get away with Mia. Just us. I want to do something for her. If I can get the villa a couple of days early and take extra leave, will you and Luke watch the boys and bring them down for the wedding?"

I have no idea if I'm going to be able to pull this off. Requesting last minute leave is one thing. I can beg Captain for that and promise to pull a few doubles to make up for it. Getting the villa a day or two in advance might be impossible. It's the beginning of the summer. A lot of people are taking vacation now. The resort could be booked up, but that doesn't mean I won't try my hardest to make this happen. Pay anything. Any amount, I don't give a shit. She needs this.

We fucking need this.

"You want to take my best friend on a mini romantic getaway? One she absolutely, one-hundred percent deserves?"

I smile, moving out of the doorway and grabbing the itinerary for the resort out of Mia's nightstand. I find the phone number on the bottom of the page.

"Fuck, yeah."

"Good. Make it happen."

mia

"ARE YOU A *wheal pwincess?"*

I smile at my first memory of Nolan as I sit on the stairs leading up to the deck, watching the boys dig around with their shovels in the sandbox Reed built them.

I'm being selfish. I know I am. Instead of seeing the positive side of this, Nolan getting two moms who will love him endlessly, I'm looking at it as a loss for me. My time with him is going to be taken from me. I'll have to share my son with someone else, someone who has more of a right to him than I ever will. Or, in my worst possible scenario, I could lose Nolan completely if he wants Angie to be his only mommy again.

My throat constricts.

God, will he? Are my worries even justified? I feel like I could be overreacting, but I don't want to be unprepared for the possibility of Nolan making that choice.

Three years ago, I met my son. This beautiful gray-eyed boy, with dimples and wild brown hair. I loved Nolan from the moment he woke me up, his sweet face so close to mine, studying me and running his finger down my nose, talking about kissing me awake in his little raspy voice. He was the cutest thing I had ever seen, with his sword and his dragon embroidered attire. He looked just like Ben. He still does. And seeing Nolan with his dad? Well, that pretty much sealed the deal for me.

Fighting my affection for Ben was impossible after that.

Nolan started calling me Mommy pretty soon after Ben and I got engaged. It was such a natural transition for him. One day I was Princess Mia, the next day I was Mommy.

Like a flip of a switch.

He didn't make a big deal about it. He didn't announce the idea or give anyone a heads up. He didn't discuss it with Ben. Nolan made a decision and went for it, waking me up with a 'Mommy, I'm hungry', and asking me for pancakes while he jumped on the bed.

I cried for a solid hour after hearing that.

I know in my heart I was always meant to be Nolan's mommy. He was my son before I met him. That won't change no matter what comes of Angie wanting back in his life.

But I'm scared. I can't help it.

I'm worried Nolan will revert back to seeing me as Ben's and not his.

I'm worried he'll go to Angie for things he normally comes to me for.

I'm worried he'll want to start calling me Mia again.

God, how will I handle hearing that? The thought coils my stomach.

I wipe at my eyes, willing myself to stop making this about me. I'll support Nolan no matter what decision he makes. And if I need to cry, he won't see it. I will never make him feel guilty.

Only love. That is all he will ever get from me.

Chase squeals, kicking his legs out and laughing when Nolan dumps a bucket of sand on his feet. Nolan repeats the action. He loves making his brother laugh.

My two boys. They're so close. They have been since Chase was a baby. I can't help but wonder how this development with Angie will affect them. They've never spent more than a couple of hours apart.

If Nolan goes back to spending days at a time with Angie, how much will they mourn each other? Chase won't understand it. And Nolan . . . I just can't see him being okay with leaving his best friend like that. He adores his brother.

"Chasey, watch!" Nolan drops down to his knees in the sand and falls over, doing a belly flop on the miniature castle he just constructed. "I'm the new king! And I'm gonna build a bigger castle on these lands! With a moat!"

Chase toddles over to Nolan and collapses next to him, laughing and yelling his little, "Na Na", trying his hardest to say his brother's name.

"Chasey, say Nolan. Nolllan. Like this. Watch me. Nolllan."

"Na Na."

"Nolllannn."

"Na."

"Chasey! You're killing me!"

I giggle, resting my chin on my fist, watching the two of them play and laugh together.

God, why did this have to happen now? I thought we had another year until I had to worry about Angie dividing our family.

I can't deal with this. Nolan and Chase shouldn't have to deal with this. She can't just . . .

Heavy footsteps behind me draw my attention off of the boys and over my shoulder.

Ben descends the stairs, his head lifted as he looks out into the yard. The hint of a smile on his lips.

He loves seeing Nolan and Chase play together. I know he missed that a lot the past two months.

He claims the spot next to me on the step, leaning forward and resting his thick forearms on his knees, pressing the side of his body into mine.

"You were on the phone a while," I say, my voice so quiet I barely hear it over the worrying thoughts corroding my mind. "Did she have a lot to say?"

"No."

His brief and exceptionally vague response peaks my attention.

My eyes narrow in on the smirk tugging at the corner of his mouth as he watches the boys. "What . . . Why do you look like that?"

He turns his head. "Like what?"

"Like you are hiding something from me." I frown. My shoulders drop a little. "Ben, what's going on?"

Christ, what now? And why would any part of this be amusing?

He grabs my hand and brings it to his mouth, kissing the back of it. "I'm taking Nolan over there tomorrow after I get off work. Their visit will be brief. Angie knows that. I don't know if she had a lot to say or not. I said my piece and hung up."

Confused, I stare at him. "Okay."

He laughs a little. "I'm not fighting a grin 'cause of that, angel. Believe me. I don't want to deal with this shit. I'd rather keep Nolan away from Angie, but I know this will keep things more amicable and in the end, it'll only benefit us. I'm sorry. Don't think I'm happy about anything involving her. I have other things on my mind I'm thinking about. Things involving you and me. I'm excited. I can't help it."

I blink.

He's excited? Things involving him and me? What things? I want to be excited about something.

Leaning into his shoulder, I glare at him, pursing my lips and fighting my own smile. "Care to share, Officer?"

"That would ruin the surprise, wouldn't it?"

"It's a surprise?"

He grins. Those two massive dimples appear.

I exhale sharply.

Sheesh. How are dimples even sexy? They're supposed to be cute. A quirky abnormality. But on Ben, they're downright lethal. Dangerously alluring. I can barely think straight when he smiles at me like this.

And him smiling right now is the only response he's giving up. He isn't going to tell me anything about this surprise of his.

Well . . . two can play at this game.

Sitting up a little taller, I steal my hand back and turn my head, looking out into the yard. "I have a surprise too. A kinky surprise. It's epic to the nth degree. Probably illegal." I smirk when I feel his eyes on me. "Not telling you anything about it either."

"When is this surprise going down?"

"Tomorrow."

I pinch my eyes shut, clenching my teeth and growling, annoyed with myself for not holding to my previous statement. A little annoyed with Ben for getting information out of me so easily.

Pathetic. I can never keep anything from my husband. Just being in his presence is like taking a shot of truth serum. And this is a good surprise! It should be kept secret.

Come on, Mia. Play the game well or don't put yourself in it.

"That's all you're getting," I promise. I actually sound convincing.

Ben leans further into me. His nose brushes against my hair. "This surprise have anything to do with that sexy as fuck slip you were wearing today when I was pushing inside of you?" he asks quietly, even though there is no way the boys can hear us right now. They are too far away and being too noisy themselves.

Still. Whispered words have a bit more indecency to them than things spoken at normal octaves. And Ben is all about the indecency.

I tilt my chin. My cheeks burn.

Damn it.

"I have no memory of such thing," I lie.

He laughs darkly in my ear. "Which part, baby? Your ass in my hands while you fucking owned my mouth, my fingers stretching you until you begged me for more, or my cock filling that tight pussy. You telling me you're forgetting some of that?" He grips my thigh. My entire body shudders. "'Cause I'm betting you remember every second of it, pretty girl. I'm betting you're getting wet right now just thinking about what we did."

Blushing, I turn my head and bring us nose to nose, expecting to see desire pooling in Ben's eyes. Hunger, but only recognizing love. Strong and steady love. That warmth he has inside of him, pouring out onto me.

His motive becomes clear.

"Are you trying to distract me, Benjamin Kelly?"

"Maybe."

"Why?"

He reaches up and moves his knuckles over my cheek. "'Cause I don't like seeing my girl upset. If I can change that, make you smile somehow, I'm going to do it. I don't want you worrying, Mia. Ever. This shit with Angie is going to be handled. I know me telling you that you have absolutely nothing to worry about with Nolan isn't going to stop you from sitting out here and thinking the worst. I see you doing it, baby. I thought maybe I could take your mind off of it for a minute. Get you thinking about something else. Did it work?"

Of course Ben plays dirty when it comes to distraction. I wouldn't expect anything less.

I couldn't appreciate anything more.

Nodding, I hold onto his wrist. "Yes. It did. Thank you."

"I don't want you thinking you're ever alone, Mia. What you feel, I feel. Anything that upsets you, tears me apart. It's always been like that."

"Always? Even before?" I ask, fighting tears again, smiling at my own absurd question and the tender look he's giving me.

Even before . . . He knows what I mean—when we both hated each other. When Ben had nothing but mean things to say to me and I had nothing but awful thoughts filling my head about him. When I associated the name Benjamin Kelly with every curse word I could think of, and he barely spoke mine without tacking on a few of them.

Did it tear him apart upsetting me back then?

I know the answer. And I know the one he's going to give me too.

Because this is Ben. My Ben. The man who convinces me every day without realizing it that my life was always his.

Even before.

"Yeah, angel," he answers with nothing but honesty in his voice, trusting those words and breathing meaning into them, enough so that I'll accept his certainty and forget the one I was sure of.

We choose to believe what we want to believe. I choose Ben. He is my truth.

Sighing, I press my lips to his, kissing him slowly and moving my fingers along his cheek.

"I love you," I breathe into his mouth.

He drops his forehead against mine. "That's all I need,

Mia. All I'll ever need."

I close my eyes.

God, what did I do to deserve this man?

Leaning back, I study his face. His dark eyebrows and the freckle under his left eye. The day-old stubble coating his jaw.

"Is there really a surprise?" I ask, poking the spot on his cheek where his right dimple appears.

He nods. "You?"

Nodding, I kiss him once more, smiling against his mouth, wanting so badly to tell him what I have planned for us tomorrow.

But I don't. And I'm not going to, as long as he doesn't ask me anything else about it.

Letting my hands fall away, I turn and look at the boys.

Chase is flinging sand everywhere and Nolan is filling up a pail.

"We should tell Nolan now, that way you aren't springing this on him tomorrow. Give him a little time to think about it. You know?"

I have no idea how Nolan is going to take hearing about Angie wanting to see him. I know he's asked Ben about her in the past, wondering what happened to her and why she isn't around anymore, but I haven't heard of him bringing her up recently.

Unless Ben isn't telling me.

"Yeah. Good idea."

Ben stretches his legs and stands from the step. He grabs my hand and tugs me to my feet, walking with me across the yard.

The boys look up as we draw closer.

Chase slowly climbs out of the sandbox, lifting one leg over the wooden ledge, then the other, teetering a bit on his feet before rushing to greet us.

I pick him up and kiss his chubby cheek. "Baby," I murmur against his skin, smelling the orange he ate an hour ago for a snack.

"Nolan. Come here a minute."

Hearing Ben's voice, Nolan hops out of the sandbox and hurries over.

"Yeah?" he asks, tilting his head up, the front of his shorts and T-shirt covered in a light dusting of sand.

Ben squats down and rests his hand on Nolan's shoulder. "Buddy, you remember Angie, right? Your other Mommy? The one you used to live with before you moved in with Daddy and Princess Mia?"

His big eyes flick to mine, then he looks back up at Ben, nodding his head.

"She wants to see you. Would you like that? Would you like to go see her tomorrow?"

Nolan stares at Ben for a moment. "Why does she want to see me?"

"Because she misses you," I tell him, smiling when he glances up at me, keeping all of my other emotions hidden and only giving Nolan what he needs to see—my happiness for him. "She hasn't seen you in so long, baby. I bet she won't believe how big and strong you've gotten."

My words don't seem to reach Nolan. Or my happiness.

Brow pinched together and his mouth pulling into a frown, his little nostrils flaring with his heavy breaths, he keeps his passive focus on Ben. "But I want to stay here. I don't want to live somewhere else again."

"You aren't living anywhere else, buddy. You're just visiting Angie. I'm not leaving you there."

"Does she want to see Chasey too?"

I shift Chase to my other hip. "I'm going to keep him home while you and Daddy go see her, okay? That way you two can talk and your brother won't interrupt you."

Nolan shakes his head. "I don't wanna go if Chasey doesn't go."

"Nolan." Ben's hand falls away when Nolan moves to stand in front of me.

"Are you gonna stop being my mommy now?" he asks, genuine fear tightening his voice.

My mouth goes slack. Any emotion I was trying to keep from Nolan comes bubbling to the surface, demanding to be acknowledged.

Squatting down in front of him, with tears brimming my eyes and my chest compressing so much I can only take in shallow breaths, I set Chase down and reach for Nolan.

"I will never stop being your mommy. Not ever. Okay?" I cup his face, wiping some sand off of his cheek. "You're my little knight. And you and Chase, you will always be my two favorite boys. This doesn't change that, Nolan. Your other mommy can love you too. We can both love you, and we can both be your mommy."

"I don't want to call her Mommy."

Ben rubs Nolan's back, briefly glancing at me while holding onto Chase with his other arm. "You can call her Angie, buddy. You don't have to call her Mommy."

I nod when Nolan looks at me, grabbing onto his hands. "Whatever you want to do."

"Can you come with us?" he asks quietly, pleading with his eyes. "Please, Mommy? And Chasey? I think she wants to see everybody."

Angie wants to see me and the son I have with her ex?

Yeah, I'm sure.

I breathe a laugh. Tears wet my cheeks. "You want me to go, baby?"

Nolan nods his head.

"Buddy . . ."

"Okay. I'll go," I interrupt Ben, smiling at Nolan and running my finger down his nose. He reaches out and does the same to me. "You want me there, I'm there."

"Cool." He looks between Ben and myself, the apprehension in his face vanishing. "Can I go play now? My castle is really coming together."

Smiling against my hand, I watch Ben rustle Nolan's dark hair. Sand falls onto his shoulders.

"Yeah, buddy," Ben chuckles. "Go play."

Nolan spins around and dashes across the yard toward the sandbox. Chase immediately starts fighting against Ben's hold, grunting until he's put on his feet. He takes off running after his brother.

Ben looks over at me. "Are you sure you're okay with going tomorrow? Baby, I can talk to Nolan. He'll be fine with whatever. You don't have to do this."

I move to stand in front of him, reaching for his arms and pulling them around my waist as we both face the boys. My head drops back against his chest.

"He wants me there. I think it'll make him feel more at ease about it if it's all of us with him. He's nervous."

Nolan thought he was leaving us. That we were sending him to live with Angie again. He looked so worried.

I'll do anything to avoid him feeling anxious about this.

"I'll be fine," I say, determined to be there for Nolan. "Whatever he needs me to do, I'll do. I just hope it doesn't involve hugging that bitch."

I can play nice, but there's a line even I am not willing to cross. She'll be lucky to get a smile out of me.

Ben laughs against my hair. His grip around my waist tightens.

We stand in the middle of the yard, watching the boys play until the telling signs of tiredness shadow their faces. After baths and story time, I escort the boys into our bedroom, not theirs.

I don't want tonight to be the night they stay asleep in their own rooms. I want them with me.

Ben gives me a questioning look as they climb up onto the bed and under the covers.

I shrug.

He smiles, nodding once, understanding my need to have them close tonight.

Usually I'm praying for a moment alone with Ben, minutes where we can grasp at each other before the boys are waking up and crying out for us.

Not tonight.

Tonight I choose little elbows poking me in the ribs and feet kicking out. Tonight I choose a restless night's sleep from a wiggling body beside me and hot breath against my neck.

Right now, nothing sounds more comfortable.

ben

H EAVY RAIN PELTS against the windshield of the
squad car as Luke drives us out of the precinct parking lot.

It's been coming down like this all day. Rain so thick the
only discernible indication of approaching traffic being the
weakened headlights slicing through the sheets of precipita-
tion. Shit conditions to drive in. Standing water on a few main
roads has caused some issues. Several vehicles have gotten
stuck. According to my weather app, it's supposed to keep up
with this intensity and continue pouring the rest of the week.

But what the fuck do I care about the weather in Ruxton
over the next few days? I'm leaving soon. Taking my woman
and getting some much needed time together.

And the forecast for Sparrow's Island? Sunny and warm.
Perfect Mia bikini weather.

Goddamn. I can not wait for this. Two days alone with my
wife. No kids. No disruptions. I get her for forty-eight hours
straight and I'm taking advantage of every minute.

I'm tasting every part of Mia. Touching every inch. Taking . . .

Stripping her of her clothes the second I get her in that
room and burning the outfits I packed for her 'cause she won't
need them. I want her in the flesh. On every surface of that
villa. Skin to skin, her soft curves pressing up against me while

I move inside that sweet perfection I'll never deserve. While I devote every second of those forty-eight hours to her pleasure. To ours. Nothing between us but our panting breaths and the space I'll allow myself to have just to fucking stare at her.

I shift in my seat a little.

Fuck, my balls are drawing up just thinking about it. I need her. This day can't end soon enough.

And before it ends, Mia will be giving me her own little surprise.

I rub at my jaw, thinking as I stare out the window. Beside us, a tractor trailer drives through a puddle. A rush of water sloshes on the hood.

What is she planning? I can't imagine it being anything related to fucking. Not with the kings of cock-block roaming the house.

She knows it's pointless.

I get hard. She slides down on my dick. Five seconds later someone cries or screams or beats their tiny fists against the door, begging and bargaining for entry. Turning the locked knob and sobbing harder when they're kept out.

Mia tenses. I'm thrown off of my game. I can't fuck my wife when my kid is crying ten feet away, when I can see his little fingers reaching underneath the door and tapping the carpet, his husky voice desperate and sad.

I also can't keep experiencing five seconds of Mia's pussy. It's torture. The worst kind.

Here's a taste of heaven. Oh, you love it here? Too fucking bad. Time's up.

For the sake of my balls and everyone's sanity, we haven't tried anything the past couple of nights. We were in agreement, both of us on the same page. Now she's throwing a surprise at me?

She said it's epic. I'd classify every surprise Mia has ever given me involving her body as epic.

The time she videoed herself masturbating and sent it to me while I was working a double. Or the time she woke me up taking half of my cock into her ass.

Christ, I'll never forget that anniversary. Filthy girl. She made me come so hard that night.

She might be as sex starved as I am, but she isn't a sadist. Mia wouldn't try and pull something tonight knowing damn well whatever we start, we won't be finishing. That eliminates anything sexual in nature. And if it doesn't involve her tits and ass, I'm stumped. It could be anything.

Maybe she's pregnant.

The idea shocks my awareness, spreading to every thought center of my brain and eliminating any and all other possibilities.

It makes sense. Mia has surprised me before with news like that. And we did have that one day last month when she managed to get Chase asleep while Nolan was at school.

I was out, dead to the world after my shift, but the second I felt her hot tongue on my cock the last thing on my mind was getting any rest.

I pinned her down and fucked her hard and fast on the floor until she came with a scream muffled by my hand. My orgasm quickly followed. Afterward, we laughed together as we admired each other's rug burns. I kissed the scarlet marks on her skin.

Holy shit. Is that it? Am I going to get home tonight and hear my angel telling me she's carrying another one of my kids?

"Fuck," I whisper, scrubbing my face.

My head drops against the seat.

"What?" Luke glances over at me. "You forget your wallet or something?"

He notches up the speed of the wipers to the highest setting. It does little to improve visibility. I can barely see the lines on the road myself.

I shake my head, ignoring the weird smirk he's wearing.

"Why are we going out to get lunch again?" I ask, gesturing at the weather. "We could've ordered in and avoided this shit. I can't see anything."

"I can see."

"Is that why you keep leaning forward?"

He glares through the windshield. "Fuck off."

I chuckle, staring ahead as he drives us into town.

Luke insisted on running out to grab something today. Arguing some bullshit about how food always tastes better when you eat it inside the establishment.

What the fuck does that matter?

Asshole. He wouldn't shut up about it. He also wasn't hearing me when I said I wasn't interested in spending any more time on the road in these conditions. We've been out in it all day. I was fine staying in, but he kept pressing.

Naming different restaurants with quick service and stunning views. Like he gives a shit about scenery. Pulling up menus on his phone and reading to me the in-house specials. I couldn't take it anymore. It was like being in the toy store with Nolan, only instead of the newest Lego kit, Luke was on the verge of begging me to go out on a fucking date with him.

He paced in front of my desk until I launched out of my seat and shoved his ass outside. I'm sure if I didn't have some muscle on him, Luke would've chosen that tactic himself.

It would've saved him a fuckload of time.

"Fucking Christ," he mumbles, sitting up a little taller.

The corner of his eye narrows.

"You can't see shit," I snap. "Pull over. You're going to get us killed."

"Anybody ever tell you you're the worst passenger ever? How does Mia stand it?"

Mia.

Desire stirs in my blood. I shift again in the seat, tugging at my slacks.

"She doesn't. I drive. Keeps me distracted from putting my hands on her."

Or distracted enough. I still have use of one hand.

Luke laughs under his breath. He shoots me a quick glance. "You're so fucking tense, man. Look at you. How close are you to yanking the wheel right now?"

My brow tightens.

Am I tense?

I'm fucking horny, and I'm anxious to find out if I'm going to be a dad again. Maybe I am being a little short with people lately. I did almost make that woman cry today when I asked her why the fuck she thought it was a good idea to try and cross a bridge with two feet of standing water on it. Then there was Richardson, that dickhead. I was ready to push his ass into traffic after interfering on my time with Mia.

Maybe I need to ease up a bit. Maybe not. All these assholes are probably getting regular, uninterrupted sex, so fuck them.

I flex and relax my fingers around the door handle, willing my restlessness to fade.

"By the way, I owe you and Tessa for agreeing to keep the boys. Anything . . . when the time comes and you need a favor, you got it."

Luke's shoulder jerks. "We're happy to do it. You know

we love hanging out with them. It'll be good for us anyway."

A nervousness changes his tone. His voice grows tighter. I stare at his profile. "You two okay?"

Shit. Am I so absorbed in my own depravity that I'm missing the signs of my family's unhappiness?

Luke cuts me a look. His eyes flickering wider. "What? Oh . . . no. I didn't mean it like that. Fuck. Sorry." He shakes his head and resumes looking forward. "We're great. She's great. It's just the whole kid thing. Tessa avoids that topic like the goddamn plague. I can't get her to talk about it."

"You want that? Kids?"

"Fuck yeah, I want that. And I thought she wanted it." He exhales noisily while adjusting his grip on the wheel. "Shit. I think she still does. I don't know. It's like she's scared to talk about it with me. Anytime I bring it up she gets fucking weird. The other day she told me she was running to the store to pick up her birth control, and I said something about maybe not picking it up. You should've seen her. She pretended she was getting a phone call and ran out of the house."

"Subtle," I laugh. "I can see her acting like that. Think about where she's coming from."

His head snaps in my direction. "I am! I get it. I get that. But fucking talk to me, you know?"

Suddenly, I'm no longer the only tense person in the car.

Luke is wearing his emotions right now. I see it shadowing his face. His honesty too. He wants kids with my sister. He wants them more than maybe he's willing to share. And he's frustrated because she's shutting him out and refusing to talk about it.

I can't say I don't understand her reaction. I know what losing Luke did to Tessa.

And she had to go through it twice.

"You want her to see you with the boys. See how relaxed you are about it," I suggest.

He nods once. A muscle in his jaw twitches. "I just keep thinking that maybe having them around will get her talking," he says, turning the wheel. "It'll be like practice for us. Our family. I don't know. Fuck it. Maybe it won't and she'll just stay locked in our bedroom over the next two days. If that happens, expect phone calls. I don't know what the hell I'm doing with your kids."

I laugh, deep rumbles sounding from my chest.

Luke gives in too and looks at me, grinning, his own tension slipping away.

"You'll figure it out," I tell him, fixating my gaze through the windshield again. "Just lock up your guns and keep Nolan away from anything that has the potential to start a fire. Even if you think, nah, there's no way he'll figure that out, trust me. He will."

"Shit," he says quietly. "He's not gonna try and shove Chase in the oven or something, is he?"

I meet Luke's anxious eyes, keeping my gaze cautious.

Nolan would never do that, but picturing my best friend sleeping on the floor in his kitchen and guarding the appliances is too tempting of an image not to build on.

"They sell all that baby-proofing shit at Target, right?" he asks, cutting his eyes away.

I keep my smile from my reaching my voice. "That's where I bought it."

He rubs at his jaw. I swear I hear him mumble something about cutting the power to his house and making everyone camp outside.

He'll be a great dad.

My thoughts fade to Mia again as the rainy drive continues.

Her full lips. The sun-kissed tone of her skin. The way her breasts jerk and sway when she's bent over and I'm filling her from behind.

I pinch my eyes shut.

Jesus fuck. I need to get laid.

The terrain beneath the car suddenly becomes rougher. I jostle a little in my seat, breaking out of my Mia haze and taking notice of my surroundings.

Luke has turned us onto a narrow access road on the outside of town. It's remote, unnoticed by those who aren't looking for it. We've been called back here before for abandoned vehicles being dumped.

Thick trees line the path. The loose gravel pops beneath the tires.

I straighten my back. "What the fuck? Are we having a picnic? What are we doing here?"

This asshole has been bugging me all day about going out to grab something to eat, and he brings us here? We're at least ten miles away from any place serving food.

"Man, what the hell?"

Luke ignores me and pulls over when the road widens. He shifts the car into park and turns to look at me. "You are so fucking hard-headed, you know that? You've been a complete pain in my ass with this and I'm only trying to help."

I stare at him. "What the fuck are you talking about?"

He exits the car without answering me, running through the rain across the small clearing and toward a red Jeep parked between two trees.

Mia's red Jeep.

Energy sizzles up my spine.

Is Mia here with the boys? What the hell is this?

I shove my door open and get out of the car.

The rain soaks my hair and drips onto my face. I wipe it from my eyes, watching Mia toss something at Luke as they pass each other.

Her keys, maybe?

She smiles, securing her coat together with her hand against her chest and sprinting in my direction, her long legs shifting fast beneath her.

"Where are the boys?" I yell, squinting through the rain.

"With Tessa!" She shields her face with a hand to her brow. "Ben, get in the car!"

The Jeep peels off, kicking water up behind it.

I look at Mia, then at the car. The back seat.

Fuck yeah.

I climb into the back seconds before she pulls the other door open and slides her body along the soft leather beside me.

The doors latch shut.

"Oh, my God. This rain is crazy," she giggles, wiping at her face and gathering her drenched hair over one shoulder.

She looks up at me, smiling. Water beads on her lashes.

"Hey."

"Hey." My breath rushes out of my lungs as I gaze at her.

She looks beautiful, wet and a little breathless from her run. Her dark eyes glowing with anticipation and her pink tongue moistening her lips. I move my knuckles over her flushed cheek and pluck the collar of her rain coat. It opens at her neck, revealing bare skin. A soft laugh erupts from her throat.

"Baby," I rasp. My cock jumps against my zipper.

"Surprise."

She slides the heavy coat off her shoulders and down her arms. It falls to the seat beneath us. Black lace and satin cling to her curves, the heavy swell of her breasts press against the fabric.

The outfit from yesterday. This is her surprise. Sex. Un-interrupted fucking in the back of my squad car, with her looking like the embodiment of every fantasy I could ever conjure up.

Christ, I'm the luckiest man alive.

I grip her waist as she straddles me.

"Goddamn, Mia."

"Did you guess?" She kisses my jaw and moves her lips to my cheek. "I hear you were being very difficult this afternoon. Poor Luke."

I watch her hands dip between us and tug at my belt.

"Actually," I begin, rubbing her sides. "I thought you were going to tell me you were pregnant."

She stills. Her head lifts and these big brown eyes grip me. "Oh."

"That's the only thing I could think of. I ruled out any-thing dealing with sex because of the boys." I smile and tug her closer. Her startled breath bathes my face. "Didn't realize my wife was so fucking filthy. This is kind of illegal, you know? You been planning this for awhile?"

Illegal. Like I give a flying fuck about laws right now.

If Mia told me the only way to get to her pussy was if I robbed a bank, I wouldn't even bother going to the next town over. I'd clean out Ruxton and deliver that bag of money in one hand and my dick in the other.

She shakes her head, shyly avoiding my eyes. "Since yes-terday." Her hand flattens against my chest and she pushes back, pressing me against the seat, putting space between us again so she can work at my slacks. "This is my fantasy."

"Is it?"

She nods, keeping her attention lowered.

"Just like this. When I finger myself this is usually what I'm thinking about."

My chest heaves.

Jesus Christ.

The scratch of my zipper sounds, then her warm hand is wrapping around my shaft and pulling me free. She pumps my erection, squeezing in slow, leisurely jerks.

I grit my teeth. My thighs tense beneath her.

"God, Mia. How do you want this? What happens in this fantasy, angel? Tell me."

I'm hoping this involves me restraining her in some way. The use of my cuffs. We've played like that before and every time Mia is perfect in her submission. Trusting, willing to take what I give her and so fucking wet I can put my mouth on her pussy and drink from it. But sweet holy fuck, I'm so turned on right now I might agree to anything. If she wants to run this, to take her pleasure from me and use my body to get off, so be it.

I'm hers.

"You're just like this," she whispers. "Fully clothed with your cock out. I ride you until we both come."

She inches closer and positions me between her legs.

No panties.

I groan when I feel the soft, plump skin against my shaft.

"*Baby.*"

"You're so hard," she moans. "God, Ben. Always. I always want this. Do you know? I think about touching you and being with you like this all the time. It's constant. I . . . think there's something wrong with me."

She bends and kisses me, dragging her teeth across my lip, dipping her tongue into my mouth as she slowly lowers herself onto my cock.

Lower.

Lower.

Fuck. Let me die here.

Pleasure ripples through her body. Through mine. That moment of our joining gripping me low in my belly, sending slivers of warmth up my spine and prickling in my scalp.

I brush her wet hair back away from her face and watch her move up and down on my dick, stretching herself wider and wider. Her desire coating my length and trickling over my balls.

"Nothing wrong with you, angel. I'm the same way." I thrust my hips a little and she gasps. Her head rolls to the side. "I ache for you. Want you so bad I can't fucking breathe."

"Will it always be like this?"

Like this—wild and vital. More than a necessity to me.

I grab her face and kiss her hard, sucking a little on her tongue. "What do you think?"

She nods, whimpering a quiet "yes" into my mouth, then leaning back to gaze at me and tugging the ends of my hair. "I ache for you too."

My response, a hoarse "good" gets caught in my throat as I watch Mia subtly rock her hips, her hands moving to my shoulders and seeking anchor there.

She alternates between grinding in my lap and bending forward so she can bounce on my dick, pressing her lips to my ear and whispering my name, telling me to fuck her.

I squeeze her ass and slam her down on my thighs.

Her moans grow louder, echoing against the glass.

"God, listen to you. Hear how wet you are?"

She whimpers, arching her back. "I need this."

"Take it. Christ, take everything, Mia."

Her wide, unsure eyes focus on mine. She blinks.

"Take it," I say again. I move my hands to her hips, holding them gently, dropping my head against the seat and giving her my body to use.

"Come on, baby. Ride my dick."

She smiles a little, biting at her lip, her dark hair conceal-ing half of her face.

I watch in amazement, in pure lust-driven wonder as Mia moves in my lap, pumping her hips and circling them, reaching back to hold onto my legs as she slides up and down my thick shaft.

Rain taps steadily against the windows, the light slipping into the car moving over Mia's body and shadowing in the slope of her neck. Sex clings to the air, that unmistakable scent of Mia's arousal filling my nose and lungs, making my dick swell inside her tight, wet heat, making it near impossible not to lose my fucking mind.

Water drips from the ends of her hair onto her skin. I watch a drop disappear between her breasts. My mouth chases after it, my tongue licking and tasting her cleavage like a man starved for drink.

"Ben," she moans.

"You're soaked." I thumb her nipple through her linge-rie. "And the way you're gripping my cock, trying to milk me . . . Fuck, Mia. You're making it real hard not to come, baby."

"Don't. Not yet. There's something else that happens in my fantasy," she says, sounding urgent, reaching to my hip and tugging my cuffs out of the case attached to my belt. She holds them between us, letting them dangle from her finger. "Put them on me?"

I growl, fighting the urge to climax at the sound of her request, plucking the cuffs off her finger and gathering her arms behind her back.

She inhales sharply.

I bite and suck on her neck, securing the metal to her wrists at the same time as asking, "Like this?" and then it's me taking her, grabbing her hips and holding her still while I thrust away from the seat, while I pound into my woman and give her every fucking inch of my cock.

"Oh, God," she cries. "My breasts. Please."

"Fuck," I groan. Sweat beads on my brow. "You want my mouth?"

She doesn't answer, or she does and I can't hear her over the blood rushing in my veins and the heavy pounding of my heart.

I slide my hand underneath her lingerie and lift one breast, then the other. They bob free, so fucking heavy, swaying a little as I continue to fuck her.

I stare, mesmerized.

"Jesus. Your tits, baby. So fucking gorgeous."

I lean forward and capture one in my mouth. Her nipple pebbles against my tongue as I suck until my cheeks hollow, until she squirms and pants in my arms, begging me to bite her and mark her skin, to suck on the other one and pinch her nipple.

"Harder," she pleads. "More."

I lick between her breasts and the hollow dip in her throat. I suck on her jaw, her lip.

She looks at me, panting, "I need you, Ben. So much."

I nod, telling her with my eyes and my hands and my lips pressing against her skin that she's not alone, that everything she feels I feel. That it's more for me.

That no one has ever loved like this.

I hold her cheek, grinding my jaw as I thrust and thrust up into her, my hips jerking in quick movements and my balls slapping against her swollen cunt.

She drops her head back. Her body jumps in my arms, and that familiar wet tightening around my cock gets me with her in seconds.

"Ben . . . oh, shit. Oh, shit. I'm gonna come."

"Mia," I groan, squeezing her waist, my stomach clenching and my legs burning as I chase after her, needing this release.

So fucking close. Right there . . .

Something sharp taps twice on the window, startling us both.

My orgasm pulls out of reach and dissipates into nothing.

Rage flashes through me. Sharp and painful in my veins. "WHAT THE FUCK?" I yell, glaring at the dark figure standing outside the car.

The glass is fogged all around us. I can't make them out.

Doesn't matter. Whoever it is, they're fucking dead.

Mia slumps against my chest and continues pulsing on my cock, taking her pleasure, whimpering against my neck as her body spasms in tight jerks.

"Oh, my God," she whispers.

"Kelly?" a voice calls out.

I snatch her coat off of the seat and wrap it around her, pulling her closer. "Motherfucker," I hiss, recognizing the voice of the man I'm about to bury. "Tully, what the fuck are you doing here?"

I watch his figure move a little. "Sorry, man. I was out here the other day. Just checking to see if the trailer that was parked back here got picked up or not. Is Evans with you?"

What the fuck did he just say?

"Do you think Evans is with me, you piece of shit? Get the fuck out of here!"

Mia laughs against my neck.

I tilt my head down. "This isn't funny, angel."

"It kind of is," she says quietly.

"What's up, Mia?"

"Tully!"

He steps away from the window. "All right! I was just saying hi. Jesus Christ. Ease up, Kelly. It's not like I saw anything."

I grit my teeth.

"I heard a little."

"I'm going to kill him," I growl, turning my head. "He's dead. You're fucking dead, you hear me?"

"Leaving now!" he calls out. "See you later, Mia!"

A door closes, then the unmistakable sound of a car driving over gravel signals his exit.

Now that no one's distracting me, getting off on my cock and moaning in my ear, I have no trouble hearing shit going on outside around us. It's as clear as fucking day.

Speaking of my cock . . .

Mia shifts her weight in my lap.

Groaning, I drop my head against the seat as her warm, wet pussy slides along my limp shaft.

Fuck, my balls. I hope this doesn't cause permanent damage.

"Hey."

I tilt my head down.

"Are you okay?" Mia asks, her full lips pinching together and then lifting into a soft, sated and slightly amused smile.

I take a moment to stare at her. My anger slips away.

Her cheeks are flushed. Her hair a wild mess of dark heavy waves, falling past her shoulders and sticking to her sweat soaked skin. Her nipples are still tight from arousal. Rosy blotches and indentations made from teeth decorate her breasts and the rise of her neck.

I didn't come? I no longer care. Look at her.

"You are so fucking beautiful," I say as I reach behind her back and quickly remove the cuffs. I rub her wrists and the bend in her arms, her biceps, soothing any ache she might have.

She falls forward, her head resting on my shoulder. Her body loose and warm.

Mia doesn't say anything for the longest time, then with my eyes closed and my hands moving leisurely over her back she presses the softest kiss to my neck and whispers, "I am so fucking yours."

I open my eyes.

Fuck.

A weight of relief settles over me, like I didn't know her life was mine or that I belonged irrevocably to her until this very moment.

I bury my face in her hair as we cling to each other. Desperate and adoring touches, our whispered words being muted further by the rain against the glass, but I still say them, and so does she.

"I love you."

"I love you. I think I want another baby."

mia

SOMETHING IS OFF with Ben.

Aside from the fact that he didn't come earlier today during our back-seat sex romp, we're on our way to meet up with Angie so she can spend time with Nolan, something I *know* he wishes we could avoid all together, and he seems to be in a decent mood.

No. More than decent. He's humming.

Humming. You know, that thing people do when they're feeling pleasant, or maybe even a little excited about something. Ben is doing that right now.

All things considered, it's very, very strange.

I'm expecting a noticeable irritation. A tense rigidness to his body or, since he's been deprived for months, that wily, concentrated look he gets when I know he's thinking in great detail about fucking me.

God, I love that look. I love dissecting it, crawling inside his beautiful brain and imagining what he's doing to me in there. Letting my own mind wander and then blushing when he notices my drifting attention.

Hard and fast or soft and slow. *What are you thinking, Mr. Kelly?*

Taking my focus off the road ahead, I glance across the bench seat and stare at the man beside me.

Ben is relaxed against the worn leather, with one hand

on the wheel and the other arm resting on the ledge of the open window. Over the low rumble of the engine I can hear the deep tones of his voice carrying out a tune. He taps his thumb rhythmically against the wheel.

I narrow my eyes.

What the fuck? He's probably backed up to his eyeballs in semen *and* he's about to spend time with this ex. Why is he so goddamn chipper?

As if hearing my own vexing thoughts, or sensing the scrutiny he's getting, Ben turns his head and gently smiles at me.

"Angel." He glances ahead, then quickly studies my face. "You okay?"

I cross my arms below my chest. My breasts bounce a little, drawing his gaze to the cleavage peeking out from my floral sundress.

Yeah. Remember these? I don't hear any humming now.

"Are *you* okay?" I ask. "You look like you're actually looking forward to this."

The thought settles over me like a dark cloud. I sink further into the seat, the relenting weight of jealousy gathering in my chest.

Does Ben actually want to see Angie?

His brow pinches together before he looks back at the road. "How so?"

"Well, let's see. You're humming for one. You don't hum, Ben."

"I hum sometimes."

I breathe a laugh. "Yeah. Sometimes. You occasionally hum after we have," I pause, whipping my head around and glancing in the back at the boys.

Chase is passed out; his cheek pressed against the side of his car seat. The beloved stuffed octopus pinned under his arm.

I turn my attention to Nolan.

He looks up from his iPad and smiles, ready to absorb my next words.

"Cookies," I blurt out, facing the front again. My face warms. "After we have cookies."

"Cookies?" Ben smirks, his brow lifting in amusement as he turns his head and locks eyes with me.

I limply shrug.

What the hell else was I supposed to say? Sex? I'm not trying to expand Nolan's already progressively building bank of inappropriate vocabulary. We've somehow managed to keep this word out of his little sponge of a brain. Shocking, I know. Especially with Ben requesting it for dinner and practically calling out for it in the middle of the night in his sleep. It's a miracle really. And I'd like to keep Nolan as innocent as possible.

At least, for as long as I can.

"I love having cookies with you," Ben jokes, grinning so big it's impossible to fight my own smile. A full-on dimple assault. He reaches across the seat and squeezes my thigh. "You thinking about having some right now?"

"I want some cookies!" Nolan yells from the back seat. "Do we have some with us? Mommy, you bring any?"

"Oh, my God," I groan, covering my face.

Nice, Mia. Way to think that one through.

"No, Nolan. I didn't bring any cookies."

Ben laughs. His touch leaves my leg. "I would kill for some cookies right about now."

I drop my hands to my lap and cut him a look.

Are you crazy?

He winks at me.

"Me too, Daddy," Nolan echoes. He kicks his legs excitedly

and looks out the window. His head drops against the seat with a heavy sigh. "I want some so bad. I might die if I don't get any."

My mouth falls open.

These Kelly boys. I swear.

"Buddy, you have no idea," Ben murmurs, glancing in the rearview mirror at his son.

I pull on the strap across my body to loosen it and lean across the seat, kissing the rough edge of Ben's jaw. "You are awful," I whisper. "And now I'm thinking Nolan shouldn't be allowed to have cookies until he's thirty. He's already talking like an addict."

"Thirty?" Ben snorts, his eyes shifting to meet mine. "Yeah, okay, angel. You're on your own trying to prevent that from happening."

"Well, what if he was a girl?" I ask, leaning back and watching his bicep flex and roll as he adjusts his grip on the wheel. "Would you encourage our daughter to go out and get cookies?"

He cracks his neck from side to side.

"Ah, see?" I point at him when he doesn't answer. "That's so stereotypical. Shame on you."

Ben shakes his head. "Huge difference, Mia. If we had a girl, or if we *have* a girl . . ." His voice trails off. He looks over at me, his eyebrows lifting to his hairline.

Waiting . . .

Wondering . . .

I bite my lip and press my back against the seat.

Oh, shit.

Like a conversational ninja, I avoided discussing this topic earlier when Ben announced his desire for more kids. And by avoid, I mean I slid off his lap and out of the squad car like I was fleeing the scene of a crime—in an abrupt haste.

One-sided climaxes could be considered a felony, I suppose. Using that argument, my discomposure was justifiable.

I mumbled something about needing to get the boys from Tessa in the midst of my mildly subdued panic. Not wholly a lie. She did have a lot of work to do.

Ben bought it. That's all that mattered.

And now I'm walking us right back into that discussion.

I gaze out the passenger window. At the trees whipping past us. I can't jump out of the truck at this speed. Even if I do manage a decent tuck-and-roll, I'm sure I'll break something.

My hands knot together in my lap. They suddenly feel clammy and cold. Somewhere between the dashboard and my knees, my eyes lose focus.

How can I avoid talking about this again? It's not that I don't want more kids. That's not it at all. Not even close. It's just . . .

The brush of Ben's fingers against my cheek turns my head.

He has shifted a little in his seat, his body now angled toward me and his elbow resting on top of the wheel. It's then I notice we've stopped moving. The truck is in park, pulled in front of a long driveway leading to a pale-blue rancher.

"Oh," I murmur, swallowing thickly. I look from the house into Ben's eyes. "We're here."

Great. I was so caught up in possible baby-talk with Ben, I didn't have time to mentally prepare for this nightmare of a meeting. Now I'm about to walk into it blind.

Anxiety builds at the base of my neck, tensing my shoulders. I quickly feel sick to my stomach.

"Yeah. We're here," Ben echoes, his gaze gentle. No longer inquisitive.

He turns his head, looking through the window, his body

suddenly taking on that stiff, agitated demeanor I'd been expecting and silently asking for this entire drive.

Reactive Ben. There you are.

He's no longer collected and mild-mannered. He's unyielding to the soft leather of the seat, refusing to form against it and glaring straight ahead, his nostrils flaring and his breaths growing heavier. Louder.

Now I'm wishing for the opposite. A composed, unconcerned man.

I don't want Ben to be worked up by this. I don't want him worrying or wondering what will possibly come of this meeting. Angie shouldn't be affecting my family, yet she is.

Damn it! What gives her the right to hold any power over the men I love?

I glare through the window. A figure moves onto the front porch.

Blonde. Bitch.

What gives her the right? Nothing. Angie doesn't have any right. She shouldn't have any power. And I refuse to let her believe she does.

A demanding possessiveness stirs in my blood.

This is *my* family. Mine. Not hers. Ben is mine. Nolan is mine. Chase is . . . well, obviously Chase has nothing to do with Angie, but still. If she even looks at him thinking anything besides how fucking cute he is, I might just haul off and deck her.

With a quick hand, I unlatch my seat belt and shove the door open, jumping down from the truck.

"Mia?"

I look up at Ben, my hand on the door, ready to slam it shut. My chest rising and falling rapidly. "What?" I snap.

He blinks. "You okay?"

"I'll be better in five minutes. Come on. Get out of the truck."

I run a hand through my hair, then brace that same hand on my hip. My fingers tapping impatiently on my dress as I turn my head and stare directly at Angie. My eyes narrow to tiny slits.

She holds my gaze for a solid second before cutting away and looking down.

Surprised to see me, bitch?

"You look sexy as hell right now."

"I just want . . . Wait, what?" My head whips in his direction.

What did he just say?

Ben smirks, unlatching his seatbelt, his eyes never leaving mine. "Sexy, angel. Looking like you're ready to throw down and claim what's yours. I'm feeling you, baby. I get it." He steps down from the truck and looks at me over the top of the seat, grinning a full-blown, heart-stopping grin, all big and beautiful.

I roll my eyes, even though I love that look. "You make everything about cookies, you know that?"

Shrugging, he steps back and grabs the edge of the door. "Hard not to, being married to the hottest woman I've ever seen."

I fight my smile, and lose.

"Love you," I tell him before shaking my head and looking away. My shoulders drop with a sigh. "No more sweet talk. I need to retain my edge."

"I'll try and keep it under control."

We both grab one of the boys, me cradling Chase in my arms, his eyes still closed and his body still slack from sleep, and Ben hoisting Nolan up onto his shoulders, letting him straddle his neck the way he likes doing.

I lead the way up the driveway, coming to a stop in front of the bottom step of the porch. I don't feel any need to go any further. This is good enough.

She is close enough.

Angie slowly moves to the edge of the railing.

I barely recognize her. She looks thinner. Her skin a little paler, her hair lifeless, her complexion dull. It's been three years since we spoke in person last, but gazing at her now it feels like it's been longer. She's aged terribly, that bitchy, smart-assed confidence she had burning inside her is vanished. Snuffed out.

Her shoulders aren't pulled back. She isn't asserting her place.

The woman in front of me is uneasy. Hesitant. She's looking down at me, but in no way is she above me.

Good, I want to think, just as an unexpected wave of sympathy passes through my body.

God, do not feel sorry for her, Mia. Think about what she did. What could've happened.

Angie looks nervously at my face, at Chase asleep in my arms, at the ring on my finger that I happily display for her, then over my shoulder, her gaze lifting and no doubt locking onto Nolan.

The corner of her mouth twitches. Her eyes water.

"Oh, my God. Look how big you are," she remarks through a small, shaky voice.

I turn sideways to look behind me.

Ben plucks Nolan off his shoulders and puts him on his feet.

He stuffs his hands into his little pockets, looking unsure, gazing up at me and then looking ahead.

Angie slowly descends the stairs. "Hi, Nolan. Do you

remember me? I'm your mommy. God, I missed you so much. I . . ."

"Daddy said I don't have to call you that." Nolan quickly moves to stand beside me. He slides his hand around my leg. "I don't want two mommies. Chasey doesn't have two mommies." With his other hand, he taps Chase's leg. "This is Chasey," he says.

I look down at Nolan, into his pretty gray eyes, feeling a mixture of pride and relief bubbling up inside me and spreading out to my limbs, my fingers and toes, filling me completely. Comfort so satisfying and sudden tears build behind my lashes.

Nolan is choosing me. He's chosen me. He wants to continue calling me mommy, not anything else. I don't have to give up that title now that Angie is back. I'll never have to give it up.

Her presence in his life, whatever it ends up being, doesn't affect mine. I know that now.

I blink my tears away, standing even taller than I did when I hopped out of Ben's truck as I focus my awareness onto Angie.

She's frozen on the bottom step, looking between Nolan and myself, lingering on the latter. Her hands trembling at her sides. Her bottom lip caught between her teeth.

I raise my eyebrow.

Try something. I dare you.

She looks away, blinking rapidly until finally fixating all of her attention onto Nolan. She grips the handrail, maybe to keep herself from collapsing. "W-Well, that's fine. That's okay. You don't have to call me that. You can call me whatever you want."

Humph. I can give him a few choice words to call you.

"Chasey can't say a lot yet. He can't really talk." Nolan slides behind my legs, then around to the other side of me.

He continues circling, dragging his hand across my skin and keeping his head down. "Mommy said I used to talk like Chasey, but I talk really good now. Even 'r's. I can say dragon and stuff. Chasey can't say that yet. He can't even say Nolan."

Angie smiles weakly. "You're such a big boy now. Do you still like dragons?"

"Yup. I like airplanes too."

"Good, 'cause I bought you something." She looks at Ben, clears her throat, then shifts her eyes to me when he remains silent. "Is it okay if I give him a present?" she inquires, looking cautiously hopeful.

She's asking me for permission? Me?

Huh. Wasn't expecting this.

I nod once.

She disappears inside the house, then reemerges seconds later, carrying a small bag.

"Here you go. I saw it and thought of you." She steps down and stops a foot away from Nolan, who is still gripping onto my leg, now with both hands. She holds the bag out. "Here."

Nolan peeks out from behind me to see her, then tilts his head up, blinking, looking at me anxiously.

"Go ahead," I tell him, knowing he really wants to find out what's in that bag.

I know my son. He loves presents.

Nolan lurches forward and eagerly grabs the gift bag, tearing into it and letting tissue paper float into the air and fall to the ground. He pulls out a hard plastic dragon, maroon in color, with spikes going down its spine and wings extended, its mouth open to show rows of pointed teeth.

"Cool," Nolan mutters, examining it, pressing a button on the back of its tail and watching the wings flap. He looks up at Angie. "I don't have this one."

"Oh, good. I was worried you had them all," she chuckles nervously, tucking some of her shoulder length blonde hair behind her ear. "It makes noises too. I just didn't have any batteries."

Nolan spins around and carries the dragon over to Ben. "Do we have batteries for this, Daddy?" he asks, holding it up.

Ben takes the dragon and turns it over, looking at it briefly before handing it back. "Yeah, we have some." He jerks his head. "Tell Angie thank you."

"Thank you," Nolan says over his shoulder. He tugs on Ben's shorts. "Can we go now?" he whispers. "I wanna go play with this."

"Wait." Angie steps closer, her voice taking on some urgency. Her hand suspends in the air. "You can play with it here. We can go inside if you want."

Nolan moves in, recoiling away from Angie, or from that suggestion. He presses the side of his face against Ben's thigh. "Daddy, please?"

"Nolan," Angie begs.

"He just said he wants to go." I stare her down when our eyes lock.

She suddenly looks agitated, her lips pressing tightly together and her gaze hardening. A faint trace of that brusque, entitled woman I first met three years ago materializing in front of me.

I almost allowed myself to believe I'd never see her again.

Shifting Chase's limp body in my arms, I move to stand beside Ben and Nolan, never breaking eye contact. "I think this was a good first visit," I tell Angie, keeping my voice even. "If Nolan wants, we can set something up again another time."

"He's been here a whole five minutes," she hisses,

breathing in deeply through her nose. She looks directly at Ben. Her hand moves to her hip. "I'd like more time."

"Did you not hear what my wife just said?" he snaps, his voice vibrating with anger. He takes a step forward, putting himself between us and Angie. "And what did I tell you on the phone? This is Nolan's choice. If he wants to leave, we're leaving. I'm not forcing him to do anything."

"Maybe if you'd let me talk to him about it, he'd change his mind and want to stay."

"You're done talking. He's ready to go." Ben looks behind him. "Nolan, tell Angie good-bye."

"Bye!" Nolan moves over a little so Angie can see him and waves with his free hand, clutching the dragon with the other.

I watch Angie's expression soften as she looks down. She smiles dimly at Nolan, barely concealing her hurt. That's all she gives him. She doesn't say anything. Maybe she can't without sounding too upset.

Oh fucking well.

Lifting her head, her chin quivers as she glares at Ben. "I'd like to speak with you." Her eyes bore into mine. "In private."

Gladly. I am so done with this bullshit little visit.

Ben turns his head, telling me with his eyes that I don't need to go anywhere. That I belong beside him. Always, wherever he is.

I'd stick around for that look alone if I thought the conversation they're about to have was suited for little ears.

I don't.

"Come on, baby. Let's go." I grab Nolan's hand, leading him away before the sharp edge of Ben's voice slices through the air.

I know he's holding himself back on account of his kids bearing witness, but even a restrained Ben is scary as hell when

he's pissed, which he is and rightly so. Angie knew what to
expect. She shouldn't be trying to assert any authority in this
situation or making any demands.

This is about Nolan. What he wants. If she cared about
him at all she would understand that.

I get the boys into the back seat of the truck and buckle
them in. Chase is still sound asleep. He's snoring now.

My funny boy. All that commotion probably put him
under even more.

I shut the door, spinning around and leaning against it,
watching as Ben gestures in my direction, looks at me, then
turns back and continues laying into a distraught looking
Angie, her hands covering her face and her head lowered.

Do not feel sorry for her, Mia. Think about Nolan.

I continue observing their exchange. I can't make out
what they're saying, but their voices are softer now. Ben no
longer looks irate. At least, not from this distance. I watch
Angie nod her head, say a few more words, then hurry up
the stairs and dart inside the house.

Turning, Ben stalks down the driveway, his long, muscular
legs closing the gap between us in half the time it took me to
reach the truck. His expression is indecipherable, all though
I'm certain he's still annoyed.

Why wouldn't he be?

I straighten off the door, ready to ask him what she had
to say when he moves into me and presses me against it again.

"Ben," I gasp.

His hands cup my face and slide into my hair. He bends,
claiming my mouth with his, swallowing the soft, breathless
plea before it dies on my lips.

"You," he murmurs, kissing me roughly. "What did I do,
Mia? What the fuck did I ever do to deserve you?"

"What are you talking about?"

"She's backing off."

"What?" I push against Ben's chest, just enough to peel his face off of mine. I look up into his bright eyes, staying connected to him, his hard body forming to my soft curves. "What do you mean she's backing off? She was pissed, Ben."

"I know. But it was you, angel. Angie doesn't want to compete with you. Hell, she knows she can't. She had all this fire one minute, trying to argue with me and telling me she deserved more time with Nolan, but then I mentioned something about you being there for him and always seeing him as your own. That shut her up real fast, baby. It was like it triggered something. She started crying. She even admitted how seeing you with Nolan tripped her up."

Ben grabs my face, dropping his forehead against mine. His warm breath tickles my mouth.

"You're fucking perfect. Perfect for me. Perfect for Nolan. She saw that. She's done. Unless he wants to see her, she's not going to push anything with our son."

I blink rapidly, trying to absorb this new information. Trying to understand it.

She's giving up all rights to him, just like that? The only child she's ever had, this little piece of her, the best thing she's ever done and will ever do, she's just going to walk away from him like he never meant anything?

"Are you serious? What the hell is wrong with her?" I yell, my own voice sounding shaky now.

I wiggle free of Ben's hold and begin pacing in front of the truck in the grass, keeping myself locked into a pattern of mindless stepping to prevent a sudden charge up the driveway.

"Baby."

I ignore Ben's voice, my head down, my hands drawn

into fists at my sides.

"She's missed out on so much of his life, and she's not going to fight for him? She's not going to at least try and make this work? Why not? How can someone be *done* with Nolan? I don't understand that."

She's sick. Disturbed. She has to be.

I would sacrifice anything for him. Everything. I would've fought for Nolan five minutes after meeting him.

"Mia, hey." With a firm hand, Ben grabs onto my elbow, halting my hurried steps and tugging me against him. His other palm forms to my cheek. "Stop. Talk to me. Why are you upset about this? This is a good thing."

Is it?

I stare into his eyes, seeking understanding, thinking about this a little longer than the second I took before I started moving around like a mental patient.

Angie isn't going to fight us. She isn't going to try and keep Nolan away from his father again. From Chase or me. She's going to let Nolan decide if and when they spend any time together.

It's his decision. She understands that now.

We aren't losing Nolan.

We aren't losing him.

My world slows. Clarity, warm and comforting, blankets me like the softest cloak.

With a shuddering breath I collapse against Ben, suddenly feeling weightless and relieved of the heaviest burden. I drop my head against his chest and bury my face there, whimpering when he wraps his strong arms around me, sliding my hands around his waist to his back and clutching at his shirt.

"I'm sorry," I whisper against his neck, standing on my toes to get closer. "I'm so sorry. You're right. I'm ruining this.

I've just been so stressed out about it, Ben. I was so worried she'd try and take Nolan from us. God, I was worried. I'm just in shock, I guess. I'm sorry."

He lifts me off the ground. "Stop saying you're sorry."

"Okay. I'm sorry."

Laughing, he presses his lips against my cheek, then slides them over my mouth.

"You ready for your surprise?" he asks.

I lean away, my feet dangling in the air. "My surprise? Now?" I inhale a quick breath, remembering his odd behavior on the drive over here. "Oh, my God. Is that why you were humming?"

"Sure as fuck wasn't because of this," he grunts, reaching over and opening the passenger door. He sits me on the seat. "But we did get Nolan."

"Yeah, we did," I reply, grinning, grabbing his shirt and kissing all over his face, sliding my hands to his shoulders as I press my lips to his ear. "I'm so happy."

"Me too, baby."

"Please tell me my surprise involves cookies," I whisper.

He groans and nips at my neck. "God, yes."

ben

“WAIT. WHAT ARE we doing here?”

Mia looks over at me after I shift the truck into park and cut the engine.

So adorably inquisitive. She still has no idea what my plans are for us, only that it involves hours and hours . . . and *hours* of me worshipping her perfect fucking body. I won't give her any more details. Not yet.

I don't need to. It'll all become clear in a minute anyway.

With her nose wrinkled and her finger tapping her chin, she stares ahead out the window, then leans close enough to whisper, "Is this where we're having sex? Like . . . in one of their rooms where they can hear us?"

I give her a hard look as I unbuckle my seat belt.

Is she fucking crazy?

"Yeah, baby. I called up Reed too. Figured he'd want to listen again."

Her eyes widen. Smiling, a quiet giggle bubbles in her throat. She brings a hand to her mouth and reaches for me with the other, wrapping her fingers around my wrist and squeezing.

"Ben, what's going on?" she asks.

"You'll see. Will you grab Chase? My hands are going to be full."

Mia looks around the back seat, no doubt wondering what

the fuck I'm talking about. It's practically empty back there.

"Um . . . yeah, sure."

I step out of the truck, hearing the shrill snap of a screen door closing.

Luke and Tessa pad down the driveway toward us while Max barrels around the yard.

Nolan leans forward and starts bouncing in his seat the moment I open the back door.

"Uncle Luke!" He grasps frantically at his harness. "Daddy, how much time do we have? I wanna show Uncle Luke my new dragon and this cool game I just downloaded. It's got the minions in it. You race them. I bet he'll love it."

I glance at Mia across the seat.

She's unstrapping Chase, her absorbing eyes drawn down to my mouth.

"You're spending the night, buddy. You and Chase. You get two nights with Uncle Luke," I answer, smiling as I lift Nolan out of the truck.

"Oh, yeah! Sleepover! Boo-yah!"

I hand him his iPad and he scurries excitedly up the driveway, yelling out for Luke.

"What?" Mia gapes at me, pulling a slowly awakening Chase against her. He rubs his sleepy face into her neck. "They are? Why?"

I grin and unhook the booster seat, holding it with one hand while I lift the bench and reveal the bags I packed and stored here earlier, unbeknownst to Mia. Two for us, along with a smaller cinch tote concealing a few personal items Mia keeps tucked in the back of her panty drawer at home.

Massage oil. Warming lube. Those sex dice she got as a gift at her bridal shower.

Suck this. Lick this. Kiss this. Fuck THIS.

Goddamn. I wanna rip into that bag right now. This four hour drive might feel like torture.

I grab the duffle for Nolan and Chase and hoist it out of the truck.

"Hey, lovebirds." Tessa steps up behind Mia. She ties her red hair back into a messy knot and reaches for Chase. "Gimme that cuteness."

Mia passes him off, then sticks her hand on her hip, glaring at me as I walk around to the passenger side. "Benjamin Kelly, would you please explain to me why we have luggage packed and hidden in your truck? What is going on?"

"You didn't tell her yet?" Tessa asks.

I shake my head, bending to kiss Mia's temple. She leans away and squints.

"Angel."

"Babe," she mocks, arching her brow. "Spill it."

Tessa shrugs, bouncing Chase in her arms. "I'll spill it."

I scowl at her, *fuck that, I'm saying it*, then turn to Mia as Luke steps up to the group. I hand him the duffle and the booster seat.

"Got the villa early. We're heading there tonight."

Mia sucks in a breath. "What?" she asks quietly, inching closer. Her cheeks warming as she gazes up at me. "You took off work?"

"Yeah."

"Is . . . is anyone else going down early?"

I slowly shake my head, laughing as she looks anxiously between Luke and Tessa, then back at me, those big, dark eyes wide with astonishment.

"Just you and me, angel. No interruptions."

"Ben, oh, my God." She hurls herself into my arms, wrapping her hands around my neck and pinning us together.

I can feel her heart pounding against my ribs. The quickness of her breath against my cheek.

"I can't believe you did this."

Closing my eyes, I stroke her back and inhale the sweet warmth of her skin. "I need to be with you," I murmur, only for her to hear.

I'd fucking scream it though. I don't give a shit who hears my desperation for this woman.

"Yeah," she says quietly, squeezing me a little tighter. "Me too."

"I'd do anything. You know that, right? Anything, baby."

Even if we couldn't get the villa, or my leave had been denied, I would've found a way to get Mia alone. I'm feeling this separation from her in my bones. My blood. Fuck, I'm feeling it deeper than that. This goes beyond anything physical.

Just like everything else with Mia. Since the beginning, what I feel for her goes deeper than marrow.

Her lips curl against my neck. "Me too," she says before leaning back and staring up at me. "What about this weekend, and the boys?"

Luke heaves the duffle over his shoulder. "We're bringing them down with us. Got their tuxes and stuff for the wedding. And don't worry. I just spent the last hour kid-proofing the house. There's baby gates everywhere. Like every ten feet. I put those locks on all the cabinets and stuff too." He shifts his gaze to me. "You know they make those things for toilets? Those latches? Why?"

"Small kids can fall in and drown. They're a little top heavy," Mia informs him, craning her neck to peek at Nolan.

He's balancing his dragon on Max's back while he holds his iPad in his other hand, some song I recognize from one of his favorite TV shows playing as background music.

I look back at Luke.

For a second, he looks absolutely terrified, his eyes broadening and fixating on Chase. His bicep trembling and the fingers gripping the strap of the duffle turning stark white.

"I'll put them on," he says quietly, looking down. "I bought six, so, we should be good. I can always get more."

I laugh under my breath.

Luke has two bathrooms in his house. Two. I can tell him one lock is sufficient per toilet. Not to mention a real fucking pain in the ass when you're trying to take a piss in the middle of the night.

Or, I can stand here and keep my mouth shut.

He wants to be a dad someday, he needs to get used to this constant state of failure and oversight.

Mia squeezes my hand. "I'm going to go say bye to Nolan." She stands on her toes to kiss my cheek, then saunters across the yard, beckoning Nolan over and crouching down to talk to him.

I turn around and start unlatching Chase's car seat.

"How'd it go with Angie?" Tessa asks.

"Good. Really good, actually. She's not pushing anything with him. Unless Nolan asks for her, she's staying away."

Still can't believe it myself.

I thought for sure Angie was going to be a pain in the ass about this, fighting me every chance she got and dragging me in front of a judge, begging for some sort of custody arrangement I wasn't going to be willing to give. Nothing was ever easy with her. She argued with me for sport.

I was prepared for her bullshit. I wasn't expecting her to yield.

I wasn't planning on Mia.

Her presence affecting Angie. Her fire. The way Nolan

clung to her like a son seeking comfort from his mother. His *real* mother.

I was a damn fool, overlooking my wife in that equation.

After working the belt through the slot, I turn around and sit the car seat on the asphalt.

"That's awesome," Luke comments, looking as happy as I am about this development. "She was straight-up crazy, and terrible to Nolan. Good riddance."

Tessa looks from Luke to me, shaking her head. "Wait a minute. Angie just rolled over, just like that? I don't believe it. She gets off on making you miserable, Ben. No way is she not going to fight you on this."

I jerk my chin and shove my hands into my pockets, my back pressing against the door of the truck as my eyes narrow in on my entire reason for every fucking thing I do.

Mia kisses Nolan's cheek and pulls him into her arms.

I look back at Tessa, shrugging. "It was Mia. Seeing her with Nolan messed Angie up. She can't compete with her."

"Well, duh," Tessa says, smirking. "I could've told her that a long time ago. Saved everyone the headache." Her eyes flicker a hair wider. "Speaking of which . . ."

Smiling, Tessa reaches behind her and pulls a photo out of her back pocket, careful of Chase in her arms. "Found this at Mom and Dad's. Thought you'd like to have it."

I take the photo from Tessa.

"I'll be back. Just going to put this stuff inside." Luke carries both car seats and the duffle up the driveway as I focus on the picture in my hands.

"Holy shit."

It's the three of us, Tessa, Mia, and myself, sitting close together on my parent's back porch, the sun shining down on us and casting our shadows on the cement.

We look young. Really fucking young. I can't be more than fourteen, fifteen, which would put the two of them close to ten.

Mia in the middle, her and Tessa with their arms over each other's shoulders and their heads tilted together, both of them with their tongues sticking out and their other hands holding up peace signs.

And me . . . fuck, I'm staring right at her. Right the fuck at her, smiling.

I'm smiling at Mia.

Fuck me.

Tessa nudges her hip against my side. "Look at you. You almost look happy to be sitting within fifty feet of her."

"Yeah," I mumble, moving my thumb over the image.

Her face is fuller, and she's wearing those red, squared-off glasses she always wore back then. The ones I used to tease her relentlessly about. Calling her a nerd and whatever-the-fuck-else I could think of just to get under her skin.

Fucking prick. No wonder she hated me.

A crazy mess of curls frame her face, spilling over her shoulders. Frizzy and unkempt, not like the way Mia wears her hair now, but fuck, it looks sweet on her here. Same with the glasses.

I rub at my jaw, still studying the photo. "I don't remember this."

"I don't either. Mom had a ton of pictures in my old bedroom she was getting ready to organize. This was the only one I found of the three of us together. And the fact that you're smiling at Mia like you love her . . . well, I pretty much had to take it."

I look at Tessa, dropping my hand and not saying shit back. Not arguing.

Who the fuck knows why I was smiling at Mia like that. Maybe she said something funny. Maybe her and Tessa were acting like complete fucking idiots and I found it amusing.

Or maybe I just wanted to smile at her a little.

Looking up, I spot Mia walking back over with Luke, who's got Nolan climbing on his back. Max is slumped on his side in the yard, looking exhausted from five minutes with my son.

I slide the photo into my back pocket. "You don't want it?" I ask Tessa.

"I made a copy for me," she says, kissing Chase's cheek when he starts waking up more and babbling.

"Thanks."

She smiles.

I look from Chase to her, remembering the conversation I had in the squad car before Mia showed up and got off on my dick.

"You and Luke gonna talk about things while we're gone?"

Tessa arches her brow, cradling the back of Chase's head. "Things?"

"Kids." I bend down, catching her gaze when she tries to lower it, when she tries to avoid this shit like she's apparently been doing with Luke. "He's not going anywhere," I state.

She blinks several times, inhaling a slow, deep breath. "He tell you that?"

"He didn't have to. I know Luke. Know him better than anyone. If he was worried about something, I'd know it. If he was unsure about you, or didn't think this was it for him, if he was having even a shred of doubt, he wouldn't have put that ring on your finger. Talk to him. You're his wife. If you want kids, if you don't want kids, whatever. You'll never know how he feels about it unless you ask him. Quit being scared."

Her lips pinch closed. She looks away, and I can tell she's thinking, hopefully absorbing my words.

I think I reach her, penetrate that layer of self-doubt she's hiding beneath her steely exterior. Maybe give her the assurance she needs to talk this out with Luke. Maybe pissing her off because I'm getting involved.

I don't get the chance to ask.

Mia joins us, wrapping her arms around Tessa and Chase. "Thank you for doing this for us. I seriously owe you."

"Anytime." Tessa jerks her head when Mia releases her and steps over a little. "Come here."

The two of them move behind the truck, talking all close and whispering with each other.

Discussing Luke? Fucking probably. I'm sure Tessa is getting on Mia for the shit I just said to her, telling me to mind my own business.

Christ. I'm only trying to help.

While they share their own private whatever-the-fuck moment, I say my goodbyes to Nolan, hugging him and making sure he remembers to listen to Luke and Tessa.

He couldn't be more excited about spending the night here. Luke has already promised him rides on his four-wheeler around the yard.

I remind him of his bedtime, which draws a funny look from Luke.

"You just told me you were allowed to stay up until ten, dude."

Nolan looks down at his feet. "Well, sometimes I can." He kicks a pebble. "Like, on special nights. This is special."

Luke pins his arms against his chest, shaking his head and huffing a sharp breath. "Everything he tells me he can do, I'm calling you to verify. I'm just going to go ahead and assume soda is a no, since he just told me he can have it."

Laughing, I rustle Nolan's hair, straightening up when the girls walk back over.

"Ready to go?" Mia asks, bouncing on her feet and looking so damn happy.

"Been ready."

I watch her give Nolan and Chase another fifty hugs and kisses, then another after I almost get her in the truck. The second her ass hits the seat she's jumping down again and pushing past me, mumbling something about already forgetting what they smell like.

"Mia, baby, it's two days. I'm not even taking you out of the state."

I grip the door, watching her press kisses all over Chase's face like she's doing it for the last time.

"I know. I just miss them already," she mumbles against his cheek. She dashes over to Nolan and pulls him into another hug.

He's ready to get his time started with Luke and begins squirming the second her arms wrap around him.

"Mommy!"

"Okay, okay. I'm going." After blowing him a kiss, she spins around and climbs up into the truck, securing her seatbelt quickly. "Close the door before I get out again," she says, rolling her eyes at herself.

I back us out of the driveway and get us halfway down the street before Mia is training her eyes ahead of her, prying them off of the figures growing smaller in my rearview mirror.

"You okay?" I ask, dialing down the volume on the radio, keeping one hand on the wheel and my eyes on the road. "I know this is our first time leaving them overnight. And with Chase being little . . . Fuck, is it too soon? I just wanted . . ."

My brain turns off the second Mia's hand brushes against the front of my shorts.

"Baby," I breathe, dropping my head against the seat as she unhooks her belt and slides closer, pressing her tits against my arm and her mouth against my neck, her hand rubbing my hard-on until I'm straining against the zipper and threatening to rip that shit right open.

"Jesus Christ, Mia."

She doesn't say a word as she slides the zipper down and pumps my cock. Doesn't say a goddamn thing as she ducks under my arm and runs her tongue over the swollen head, licking my slit. Her hand wraps around the base as she works her mouth up and down my length, wetting it and moaning, her lips vibrating against my sensitive flesh.

I stop at a red light, gazing down into my lap. I brush her hair out of her face and watch her work my dick.

Her lips stretching wide. Her eyes closed in pure fucking bliss.

Christ, how lucky am I? Road head? She's going to make me come so fucking hard doing this.

"That's sexy as fuck, baby."

She smiles a little around my shaft. The tiniest twitch of her lip.

Her other hand pushes inside my shorts and cups my balls, rolling them in her palm as she takes me to the back of her throat and gags, her saliva pooling in the corner of her mouth and dripping down my length.

The sight of her taking all of me is exquisite.

I gasp and fist her hair. My thighs tense against the leather seat.

"Ah, fuck, Mia. *Goddamn* . . . you want it, don't you? You want to taste my cum. Can't wait 'til I get you in that room and on your knees, can you, baby?"

"Nm, mmm."

"Fucking greedy. My greedy wife needs it. Needs my cock filling that hot ass mouth."

Her teeth gently press into my skin. Her warm tongue soothes the sting, lapping the reddened veins.

My hips start jerking, quick thrusts into her welcoming mouth.

The car behind me beeps. I know the light has changed, but I don't give a fuck.

I'm not stopping. Mia sure as shit isn't stopping. She's going at me like I'm her last meal, the last thing she wants to consume before leaving this earth.

She's choosing me. My cum. My throbbing cock.

I'm supposed to deny her just because some dickhead behind me has places to go? Fat fucking chance.

I slide my hand down her back and squeeze her ass, eliciting a little gasp from her. My other hand is in her hair, a tight fist guiding her up and down, moving her mouth along my dick as I thrust and thrust away from the seat, arching my back and growling, the nerves along my spine crackling with energy and heat and *fuck* . . . she squeezes my balls again at the same time as deep-throating me, her other hand jacking me off violently into her mouth.

"Fuuuuck, baby," I moan, emptying myself down her throat, coming so fucking hard my foot slides off the pedal and the truck lurches forward.

"Fuck!"

I shift my foot back to the brake, gripping the wheel with both hands as I continue exploding.

Mia swallows, licking and sucking me dry, making these hot, little squelching noises with her mouth.

I sag against the seat. I nearly pass the fuck out.

She purrs, clearly proud of herself. With the sexiest, sweetest smile, Mia turns her head and gazes up at me through those long, dark lashes. Her eyes soft and adoring.

"Good?" she asks, resting her head on my thigh, her breathing irregular.

Another car lays on the horn behind us. The light apparently changed again. I ignore them, along with every other motherfucker out here on the road.

My wife just sucked my brains through my cock. I'm going to love on her a little. They can go the fuck around me.

I scoop Mia up and pull her into my lap, kissing her jaw and the sensitive skin beneath her ear.

"You are going to get fucked so hard, Mia Kelly," I whisper, loving the little shudder that ripples through her body and the pause in her breath.

She presses her lips to my cheek.

"Good. Now hurry up and get us there."

❧

I TRAIL BEHIND Mia into the villa, carrying our bags and the welcome basket we received at check-in.

Chocolate, assorted teas, a bottle of wine, and some information on the resort; a map and a few local restaurant menus.

I look up after kicking the door closed.

Mia stops beside the bed and bends over, unhooking the strap on her sandal. The hem of her dress rides up.

Restaurant menus? They might as well go straight in the fucking garbage. I'm staring at my next several meals right here.

"Wow. This place is beautiful, Ben." Mia tosses her shoes against the wall and explores the ocean-front room. She runs her hand over the bedspread and fingers the amber-tinted jewels hanging from the lampshade on the table before popping into the bathroom. "We have one of those giant soaking tubs!" she yells.

Laughing, I set the bags down, all but one. I carry the small cinch tote over to the bed and pull off my shirt.

"Oh, my God, it's huge!"

I smirk. "Thank you."

Mia peeks her head out, grinning. Her eyes burn over my bare chest, then fall on the tote. "Whatcha got there?" she asks, padding across the room.

I loosen the string and pull out the oil.

Stopping beside me, Mia stares at the bottle in my hand. Her lips part with a slow inhale.

"I want to give you a massage."

She lifts her gaze. Her pink tongue wets her lips. "Okay."

"I want you naked."

Mia smiles a little. "Okay," she says, her voice softer.

An anxious whisper that makes my dick jump.

I jerk my chin at the bed. "And I really want you to lie still and let me do this. Let me take care of you." I bend to kiss her mouth. "That means no grabbing my junk."

"What?" she laughs against me. "Not even a little?"

"Not until I'm done making you feel good."

"But . . . that makes me feel *really* good."

"Mia," I growl, plucking at her dress.

"Okay, okay. No touching your junk." She kisses my jaw and waves a dismissive hand. "Jeez. You act like I can't control myself around that thing. I'm not even sure I *want* to touch it."

I arch my brow. She giggles, playfully elbowing me in my side.

Taking my silent instruction, Mia strips off her dress and

panties and climbs onto the bed, settling on her stomach. She braces her weight on her elbows.

Turning her head, her bold eyes follow my hands as I unbutton my shorts and lower them to the floor with my boxers.

She stares at my cock, unashamed in her desire. Warmth blooms in her cheeks.

"Yeah, you don't want to touch it," I joke, kicking my clothes to the side.

Mia drops her head. A soft laugh ripples through her body. "I'll never forget the first time I saw it. It kind of scared the shit out of me. I'd never seen one that big before."

I stare down at my cock, all nine glorious inches of it. My chest swells with arrogance.

Good.

"I was scared too," I tell her, climbing onto the bed and straddling her thighs.

She looks at me over her shoulder, eyes curious.

"I didn't want to hurt you. I was really hoping I'd give you this phenomenal experience and you'd only want my dick from then on out. I felt like you were mine that night. Already. The second I saw you in the bar, I felt it."

She blinks, those dark irises swelling. "I was yours," she says, sounding like she's always believed it. Maybe even as much as I have.

I swipe her hair off her face. I bend to kiss her shoulder. "Lie down, angel."

She flattens out on her chest, tucking her arms against her sides. Her cheek presses into the mattress.

Flipping open the cap on the oil, I pour a generous amount onto my palm. A few drops spill onto her skin, following the curve of her waist and saturating the comforter.

Starting at her hips, I smooth my slippery hands up her

back to her shoulders and down again, moving the oil over her body and warming it.

Her skin begins to glow. A rich scent fills the air.

Vanilla.

I massage the tops of her thighs and her ass, those sexy as fuck dimples at the lowest point on her back. She moans softly when I spend some extra time there, moving my hands lower, my fingers brushing down her crack and dipping between her legs. I push my thumbs together and press up the line of her spine.

My cock bobs heavily. The tip wet with oil.

Mia smiles, wiggling her ass a little, her eyes closed in bliss.

I know she feels me growing hard. I can't say I'm deliberately trying to rub my length over her skin. I can't say I'm not either.

"Feel good?" I ask, my hands squeezing her waist.

Feels fucking great to me.

"Mm." She nods a little. "So good. I'm so relaxed."

"Good. Turn over for me. I want to do your front."

Mia flips, stretching out on her back and smirking when our eyes lock. Her hair creates a dark halo around her.

"I bet you do," she says through a chuckle.

"You being cute?" I ask, watching her smile grow.

"Yep."

Her confidence is precious. It's deserved too. I want to do a lot to her front.

I don't waste any time. I reach for the bottle again and this time, pour the oil directly onto Mia's skin, over her perky tits and lower, where I know she's growing wet.

With a shuddering exhale, she gazes down her body. Her eyes roll closed when I begin kneading her ample flesh.

"Ben," she gasps, arching off the bed. Her legs jerk beneath me.

The pressure of my touch increases. My cock lengthens another inch. It's throbbing now. I fight the commanding urge to stroke it.

Not yet.

The longer I touch Mia's breasts, the harder I become. I try and distract my mind by forcing my hands to other parts of her.

I rub her shoulders and her biceps. Her wrists and fingers. I move to the side and work my hands down her legs.

She makes quiet, approving noises when I rub her feet. I stay there until I'm mad with lust and my cock is no longer dripping oil, but cum.

I need to take her soon.

After several minutes of focused massage, I'm back to my obsession. I pour more oil over her body and drizzle some onto my hand.

She's so slick now. Puddles pool in her cleavage and the dip in her throat. Her navel. Her skin glistens exquisitely.

I squeeze her right breast between my hands, manipulating her flesh, rolling her nipple under my fingers before giving the other one equal attention. I press the two luscious mounds together and push them higher. Oil drips down her neck.

Her breathing quickens and she starts to tremble and pant. The seal of her thighs grows tighter.

My discipline evaporates.

I reach down and stroke my shaft, spreading oil over myself and rocking into my fist. My stomach clenches. I let myself moan.

"Ben, please," Mia begs, reaching with needy fingers, grasping at my thighs and staring at the leisurely pace of my hand. She wets her lips. *"Please."*

I shift us both and spread her legs, lifting her hips off the bed and impaling her in one brutal thrust.

"Oh, God!" she yells. Her hands reach out blindly above her head, seeking anchor.

My entire body shudders. A deep, trembling moan vibrates in my chest.

"Mia . . ."

I gather her against me so she's no longer on her back, but clinging to my body instead, her legs wrapped around my waist and her fingers in my hair, tugging as I lower her.

An inch. She gasps, moaning when I lift her and start again.

More, half of my length inside now. Then the rest.

Her head hits my shoulder with a whimper.

We're both slippery from the oil, but my cock is coated in Mia's desire. I can feel the difference, her warmth on my shaft as her pussy grips me. The walls of her sex pulsating and growing wetter.

"You feel so good," I whisper, digging my fingers into her hips and bouncing her steadily in my lap.

She moans into my mouth. Her tongue sweeps inside, flicking against mine and coaxing me to kiss her harder, to take her mouth like I'm taking her body.

Savagely.

I guide her head to deepen the kiss. My pace grows more desperate, the rough slapping of our bodies coming together urgently now as I bring her down at the same time as bucking my hips.

I grunt with each thrust.

"Touch yourself," I murmur.

Mia trembles as she slides a hand between us and strokes her clit, obeying me without pause. Her fingers brush against my shaft.

"Fuck," I growl, breaking away from her mouth to look between us, keeping her impaled on the head of my cock.

"Fuck, that feels so good. Don't stop." I kiss her cheek and her jaw, my lips staying pressed to her skin. My breathing ragged. "Goddamn, angel."

She wraps her hand around my base and jerks me off into her pussy.

My spine tingles. "Mia, *fuck.*"

"I'm close," she says, her voice shaking and her head rolling to the side.

I keep one arm wrapped around her and bring my other hand between us to rub her swollen clit. The second I touch her she goes off, her cunt squeezing the tip of my cock and bringing on my own orgasm.

"Ben, oh, God," she pants, twitching in my arms. "Come. Come in me."

I groan as she milks my cock with her skilled little hand, emptying every drop inside her.

Draining me dry.

When I finish we collapse together on the bed, our bodies still joined and our hands still roaming with that hunger we can't ever seem to satisfy.

I'm not sure I ever want to.

She bites my neck and squeezes my ass. I kiss and lick her tits.

Mia gasps, kicking her feet out when I scoop her up into my arms and lift her from the bed.

"Bath time?" she asks excitedly, pressing kisses to my cheek as I carry her across the room. "I totally touched your junk," she whispers.

I throw my head back with a laugh. I kiss her sweet smile, murmuring against her mouth.

"Fuck yeah, you did."

mia

CLOSING MY EYES, I drop my head back against the lip of the tub and stretch out in the water.

My toes curl around the jets built into the side. My hands splay across my stomach, though I think if I were to let my arms go weightless they'd float up to the surface and stay there, bobbing lifelessly.

I feel so light and pliable. My limbs slack. Every muscle in my body loose and wonderfully stretched.

Courtesy of vacation sex with Ben. It's been a real fuck-fest in this villa.

Tables have been turned over. Pictures now hang crookedly on the walls.

You'd think we were trying to set some sort of world record. We've been on each other like our plane is going down.

Sighing, I smile as the bubbles fizzle and pop against my chest. The scent of lavender clutches at the air. It's soothing, and reminds me of the lotion I slather onto Chase's skin after his bath every night.

God, I miss the boys. I wonder what Tessa has them doing right now?

Heavy footsteps smack against the tile.

I peek my eyes open to see Ben standing over me, his phone in one hand and an ice bucket in the other. The neck of a wine bottle sticks out of the top.

"You trying to get me day drunk?" I ask, eyeing up the bottle after he sets the bucket on the ledge of the tub.

Moscato. Yum.

He grins, those beautiful dimples caving in his cheeks. "Maybe a little tipsy. You're hot as fuck when you get like that."

"I am?"

I search my memory for the times I've been 'a little tipsy' around Ben. I can probably count those occasions on one hand. I'm not much of a drinker.

Hmm. Maybe I should start if he gets that much pleasure from it.

"Yep." His eyes lower to the bath water. "You're hot as fuck like that too. Just saying."

I splash him. He takes a step back, amused, then sets his phone on the counter next to the sink.

"Who did you call?" I ask, drawing my knees closer to my body.

Ben reaches over his shoulder and grips his shirt, peeling it off. He tosses it onto the floor. "Reed. Asked him how much it would cost me to give you one of these tubs at home. Wanted to know if he could help me install it."

I gape at him. "What? You did?" I sit up as he looms closer. Water sloshes against the sides of the tub.

"Why?"

He lifts the wine from the bucket, pulling a corkscrew out of his back pocket and jamming it into the top of the bottle, twisting it. "Why?" he asks, looking down at me. "My wife has been spending our entire vacation doing two things, riding my dick and soaking her beautiful body in here. You can't tell me you wouldn't want one of these at home. This is your fourth bath since we got here, Mia."

I blush instantly. "Actually, it's my fifth."

His eyebrows shoot up.

"I drew one last night after you fell asleep. I'm not proud of it."

"You took a bath in the middle of the night?"

Nodding, I sink back against the tub. My eyes lower. "Yep. I think I might be somewhat addicted at this point. It just feels so nice in here."

Ben chuckles, low and deep in his throat. He pops the cork and holds the bottle out for me to take.

"You being addicted to taking baths works for me. Just means I'll get to see you naked more."

"So, it's doable? I can feed my addiction at home?"

He nods, standing taller, looking all too proud of himself and the reaction he's getting from me.

This is fantastic!

My excitement is barely containable. I do a little dance in the water, shimmying my hips along the sleek porcelain and bopping my shoulders, the wet ends of my hair sticking to my neck.

I hold the bottle with both hands and lift it to my mouth for a taste.

It's fruity and sweet. Just my style. And strong. *Wow.* My head feels a little foggy after one generous swallow.

Smiling, Ben watches me lick the wine from my lips. "Good?" he asks.

I reach for him. "Yep. Get in and let me do inappropriate things to you with my mouth. I'm feeling frisky."

Lust swells in his eyes. He quickly drops his shorts. No boxers.

Boom. Like a mic, I'm surprised that gorgeous appendage doesn't hit the floor.

Neither of us have been wearing much of anything

besides each other since we got here. It's no surprise to me Ben went commando to run to the ice machine.

It's also no surprise how wet I'm getting, even under water.

Sheesh.

He climbs into the tub and settles across from me, leaning back, his knees poking out from the water as he keeps his long legs bent and parted, allowing me to move mine between his.

I rub my feet against his strong thighs, taking another several sips of the wine and smacking my lips after it goes down smooth.

"I want to talk to you about something before you get too drunk to remember it."

Giggling, I tilt my head. "Better hurry up then. I'm already starting to feel a little bold. Like, I want you to fuck me on the balcony kind of bold."

Ben stares at me, clearly not on board with that idea. His gaze hard and unrelenting. "Not happening," he grunts.

"Or, fuck me in the ocean kind of bold."

A devious smile stretches across his mouth.

"Really? You're okay with that?" I ask skeptically, taking one last sip of the wine before dropping the bottle back in the bucket.

The ice cracks and crunches against the weight of the glass.

Since when did Benjamin Kelly become an advocate for public sex? First the dressing room, now he's eager to slide into me while we float around in the water with everyone else at the resort?

Really?

What's next? A live peep show for the wedding guests? One starring me and Mister Nine Inches himself?

Who is this man?

Ben shrugs his shoulders. "Ocean is too murky for anyone to see anything they shouldn't be fucking seeing. Not very deep, but I could make it work."

Ah, okay. That makes sense. Still an element of privacy there.

"Balcony?" He snorts, shaking his head. "No fucking way. We're not secluded, Mia. Anyone could walk by and get an eyeful of you."

"Not if I keep my clothes on."

"No."

"No . . . to clothes?"

He cocks his head.

"What?"

"Who do you think I am?"

Laughing, I slouch further into the tub, the haze of alcohol working its magic and loosening my tongue.

"Benjamin fucking Kelly. My entire world."

He grins.

"And the sexiest cop ever. Making women want to commit felonies and shit."

His shoulders jerk with silent laughter.

I narrow my eyes, digging my toes into his legs. "Something funny?"

"That mouth." His gazes lowers, hovering on the subject in question. "You're getting tipsy."

I blink at him, my eyelids fluttering slowly.

He's right. I am already buzzing a little off the wine. Five, six sips, was it? That didn't take long at all.

He thinks this version of me is hot? Interesting.

I feel Ben's hands wrap around my ankles under the water. His grip adjusts, fingers rolling, and soon his thumbs are gliding over my skin, a gentle pressure he runs down the tops of my feet and back up, fluidly repeating the motion.

My toes curl.

Sweet mercy. His hands are magical.

It feels so good my head flops back. I allow my eyes to slip closed, listening to the sound of my slow, steady breathing. I'm so relaxed I could fall asleep.

"Do you not want more kids with me?"

On second thought . . .

My next gulp of air gets caught in my throat. I open my eyes and see Ben staring at me, his expression gentled. Those bright eyes clouded by some worrying thought.

He looks despaired.

I've seen this look on Ben before. One other time I've seen it.

Last summer, when I had the cancer scare. When we spent hours and hours waiting for results, the anticipation eating at us both but ripping Ben apart, slowly consuming him from the inside out. Stripping him of his strength.

He was struggling to hold onto even the tiniest shred of hope, and every time I looked at him, it was like we had already received our answer and the nightmare was real.

These were the eyes staring back at me all those months ago. When I walked outside and overheard him saying he couldn't live without me, that he *wouldn't*, and he glanced up, pinning me to the ground where I stood ready to collapse.

It broke my heart then. It's breaking it now.

I slowly sit up. Tears bead on my lashes. A jarring pain pits in the center of my chest. A pain so agonizing I begin to feel it everywhere.

In my bones. Spreading in my veins. I feel sick and blistering angry with myself.

God, Mia. Look what you did.

My reaction is justified. Earned. This is on me. I've been the one evading, making Ben come to his own conclusions because I've been too chicken shit to talk about things. Because I wasn't ready.

Because I was afraid.

"No, I do," I whisper my answer, gripping the sides of the tub and pulling my weight, sliding along the bottom to get closer.

I need him closer.

"I do want more kids. I want so many kids with you. That's not it."

"Then what is it?" He guides me into his lap, stroking my cheek with his knuckles as his eyes search my face. "What, Mia?"

"I just don't want you to go crazy."

Ben leans back a bit. He looks baffled. "What? Why would I go crazy?"

"Because we'll never be able to have sex!"

His eyes go round, hold my gaze for several anxious seconds, then close completely as he drops his head back, a deep, rumbling laugh erupting in his chest. One so thick and rich it tickles my belly as I stay pinned against him.

Why is his sanity amusing? I'm completely lost here.

"Jesus Christ, baby." Ben grabs my face with both hands and kisses me.

Hard.

Maybe it's the alcohol. Maybe it's his stellar mouth, but I actually sway a little when he pulls back.

Whoa.

"I really thought you had some terrible shit to tell me. Like health related. It was stressing me the fuck out. I knew you were avoiding me. Figured it had to be something awful keeping you quiet. Fuck." He kisses me again. "I should bend you over right here and spank the shit out of you for that."

Now my eyes are the ones going round.

I squirm in his arms, flattening my hands against his chest and pushing when he tries to position me over the side of the tub.

"Wait a second!"

"What?" he growls, leaning in and licking my neck.

A shiver crawls up my spine. My legs fall open.

Shit. Stupid body betraying me.

Focus, Mia!

Locking my arms, I grip Ben's shoulders and force him to look at me.

He must see the seriousness in my eyes, the plea there for conversation, because he leans back, surrendering to this, to me, lifting his elbows out of the water and resting them on the edge of the tub.

He looks approachable. Ready to talk.

I dive right in. I can't afford to waste any time. He isn't the only one looking forward to that spanking.

"You will go crazy, Ben. You will. We're already struggling to find alone time together, and it's just Nolan and Chase. Do you really think adding more kids to the equation will work in our favor? You know how demanding babies can be. We'll never see each other. Our sex life will consist of both of us getting off on our own time. And knowing our luck, you'll probably get switched back to night shift again. I mean, don't get me wrong, phone sex with you is amazing and everything, but *you* can't live off that. No fucking way. Not unless you're ready to start jacking off at work."

He smiles roguishly.

I sit up a little straighter, letting my hands drop into the water. "Oh, my God. Are you already doing that?"

Seriously? And I'm not getting video messages? Not cool.

The compliant Ben, the one yielding to me slips away, evaporating into the air around us. Possessive, demanding Ben reaches out, wrapping his thick arms around my waist and turning me in his lap, pinning my back to his front, his legs sealing mine together as he encases himself around me.

I go without a fight. Truth is, I'm just happy he isn't looking hopeless anymore. I never want to see Ben look like that again.

"What did I say to you at Luke's before we left?" he asks, his mouth moving close to my ear as his chin rests on my shoulder.

I shake my head, pulling my knees in. "I don't know."

"I told you I would do anything, Mia. Anything. That will never change no matter how many kids we have. If I have to work extra shifts so I can sneak you away once a month just so we can have some time together, I'll fucking do it. Or if you want to start meeting me at that spot and letting me take you in the back of my squad car, baby, just say the fucking words. I'll set it up and make sure no one comes within twenty miles of us. We won't be getting interrupted again."

"But, night shift? Ben, it nearly killed us."

"Nearly killed us?" He grabs my chin and turns my head, forcing me to look at him. "Christ, did I bitch that much about it? I mean, yeah, it was a hard two months, with unbelievable timing on account of the boys, but it could've been two years, Mia. I'll put up with anything if it keeps me coming home to you. Big fucking picture, angel. You know? You're what I'm living for. Our family. Let them put me on night shift again. I don't care. I told you, I don't need sleep. If we have a second to be together, I'm fucking taking it. You get the boys down and you want me? You come wake my ass up. Ain't nothing killing us, baby. Ever. Don't ever think that."

He brushes a tear from my cheek, sweetly cradling my face in his hand. "I know I'm crazy when it comes to you. I know how I get when I've gone days, or shit, fucking hours without feeling you against me. I can't help it. You're in my blood, Mia. You always were . . . even before."

I gasp, sending more tears down my face.

Even before.

"Sharing Nolan with you means everything to me. And you giving me Chase, seeing a little piece of you in this life we created together, there is nothing like that, baby. Yeah, kids are demanding, and it'll probably be hectic as shit with more of them running around the house, but we'll figure it out. And if you need help or a break, if you need *me*, you'll get it. Anything, Mia."

"You really want more diapers and middle of the night feedings? You're okay with that?"

Ben smiles, pushing my wet hair off my forehead. "Yeah. I'm okay with that. This might sound really fucking corny, but I kind of feel like I'm making the world better by giving it more of you." He shrugs, looking down. "I know it makes me better."

Oh, my God. This man. My heart will never hold all of my love for him.

I turn my body so fast water sloshes out of the tub and onto the floor.

My hands wrap around Ben's neck, his snake around my waist and move lower, cupping my ass and pinning me against his rapidly growing erection, which he so sweetly grinds against my clit.

Such a gentleman. He's going to get laid so hard.

We both groan the second our mouths collide, teeth crashing together and tongues desperate for dominance. It's sloppy and chaotic and real. Our passion. Our fire. How we seem to be clutching and clutching at each other as if we're both too afraid to let go.

I know I'll never forget this moment for as long as I live. That when I'm missing Ben when he's gone, day or night, this will be a memory I go to.

"Angel," he moans, kissing a line from my jaw to my ear, his hands roaming hungrily over my body. "We really doing this? You stopping those pills?"

"Yeah. We're doing this."

"*Fuck.*"

Ben's voice, the longing in it, the desire, stirs something wild inside me.

I become frantic, mad with lust and love and want, clinging to and climbing all over his body like some sex-crazed spider monkey, taking my pleasure from him in any way I can and giving it how I know he needs.

I straddle his thigh and rock my hips, grinding on his leg as he licks and sucks on my neck, his hands exploring my ass, my breasts, and mine exploring him, with leisurely pulls under the water.

"I want everything you want," I whisper in his ear. "I always will, Ben."

"Angel," he moans again, repeating his nickname to me as he moves his mouth to my breasts, burying his face there and dipping his tongue between my cleavage. He trembles when I cup his balls. His breath hitches. "*Angel.*"

Angel . . .

I go perfectly still.

Oh, my God. How did I forget?

"Mia?"

Pushing to my feet, I stand in the tub in front of Ben, the lavender-scented suds dripping down my body and into the water. I wipe some excess foam off my breasts, my stomach, and lower, where I want Ben's attention.

On the skin just above my hip.

His eyes flicker wider when he notices it, and he leans in, grabbing onto my waist with one hand while his other swipes the bubbles from my flesh.

I watch him study the scripted black word marking my skin.

Temporarily, of course.

"Holy shit," Ben mutters softly, running the calloused pad of his thumb over the tattoo and staring at it intently. He lifts his head, gazing up at me. "Where did you get this?"

"Tessa. She found it at some store and bought it for me. I stuck it on when you went out to get ice. Hey, careful."

I grab his wrist to stop him from rubbing over my flesh anymore.

It's like he's in some sort of a trance, his fingers moving at their own volition as he stares into my eyes.

"I don't want it to come off yet. I only have the one."

I bite my lip when he doesn't say anything back, just continues looking between the tattoo and my face. His eyes unreadable.

"Do you like it?" I ask nervously. "It matches yours. Well, not the word, obviously, but it's in the same spot."

The same spot as my name above Ben's hip.

I love that spot. Love pressing against it with the tips of my fingers when he's thrusting in and out of me, or laying kisses on it when I'm teasing him with my hands. I love the way my name stands out against his skin, the three letters heavily out-lined in harsh black ink.

It's beautiful and intimate. Best anniversary gift ever.

Ben glances up at me once more, then leans closer, so close I can feel his lashes on my skin. "This." He kisses the word, his nickname for me. *Angel.* "This is so fucking sexy, baby. Jesus, you have no idea. My balls feel ready to explode just staring at you."

My head drops back with a moan when he flicks his tongue against my flesh.

"Don't just stare then," I whisper urgently, sliding my fingers through his short hair and tugging on what I can. "Take me."

He growls, standing from the water at the same time as lifting me, guiding my legs around his lean waist and cupping my ass.

Our mouths come together in a harsh, brutal kiss. The kind of kiss that leaves you dizzy and breathless, but still yearning for something else, just a little more, another taste.

An addict is born. Or in my case, an addiction is fed.

Heat, slow moving and scorching, burns under my skin and through my veins as I'm carried out into the room and lowered onto the middle of the bed.

Ben settles over me, kneeling between my legs, gathering my hands together and securing them over my head with one of his wrists. His grip is firm.

I gasp, but I don't struggle. I know this game.

I fucking love this game.

His other hand ghosts over my body before disappearing between us. After searing my mouth with another rough kiss, Ben ducks his head and sucks on my neck, moving lower over my slippery skin until his warm breath tickles my breast.

A loud, guttural moan tears through my body when

two fingers enter me, pumping in and out of my slick heat in practiced rhythm while his thumb shuffles over the smooth rise of my clit, only relenting when I tighten and swell.

It's exquisite torture. The build, then the pull away. That beautiful battle between anticipation and fulfillment.

And Ben Kelly is a master at it.

I become delirious, thrashing about on the bed, begging for use of my hands so I can touch and stroke, so I can reach out and feel the wild pace of my lover's heart.

"Please . . . let me. Fuck! I wanna make you come. Let me hold it. *Please.*"

He doesn't release my hands, but he does remove his.

I whimper when Ben's touch leaves me, drawing my eyes down the line of my body.

He catches my gaze, giving me the sexiest smirk I've ever seen him wear. Equal parts stunning and calculating. Then, holding my eyes captive, making sure I'm watching his every move, he takes the two fingers he had inside my pussy and uses them to rub my own arousal onto my left nipple. Then my right.

My skin glistens.

"Ben!"

I arch off the bed when he sucks on my breasts, tasting the skin there before moving lower.

My hands are freed.

He trails kisses over my ribs and my stomach, my hips and the tattoo, where he lingers, whispering his love for me. His hands push my legs higher as he spreads his beautiful body between them, dropping my knees over his thick shoulders and leaning in.

"You want this?" he asks, dragging his tongue sluggishly over my clit.

I answer with a moan, closing my eyes and guiding his hands to my breasts again.

The pleasure is unbelievable, the way he makes love to me with his mouth, going from slow and soft to a man unrestrained, fingers digging into flesh and pace hurried.

Hungry.

One orgasm isn't enough. Over and over I cry out as my muscles tighten in ecstasy, as the skin between my legs grows tender from his perfected assault.

I claw at his arms, his shoulders, tugging him up my body when I need my next release to happen with his.

Reaching between us, I position him at my entrance and latch onto his mouth.

He drives forward, swallowing my moans and the quiet pleas from my lips, the ones I always say when he's moving inside me.

More and *please* and *harder* and *don't stop*.

"Never," he tells me, flexing his arms on either side of my head as he bottoms out again and again, as he gives me all of his love and his life.

Sweat replaces water, beads of perspiration building on our skin as we taste and touch and take, giving it up again and again. On my knees, in his arms, up against the wall beside the bed. Ben pounds into me or I grind against him, pushing back, always matching his desire with equal desperation.

Heart for heart. Soul for soul. I am his, and he is mine, in this life and the next.

We crawl to the edge together one last time, my body breaking apart through another surge of pleasure as Ben moans my name with each thrust of his hips, his cock swelling inside of me and his body trembling.

"*Baby*," he rasps, filling me and letting go. Giving me all of him. "Again."

I smile against the wild flutter of his pulse, feeling so small in his arms, so loved and adored.

Feeling it all.

"THIS IS MY favorite song!"

Laughing with my head on Ben's shoulder and Chase in my arms, I watch Nolan spin around in the middle of the dance floor at the resort tiki bar, shaking his little hips in tune with *Fireball* by Pitbull, as it plays through the speakers surrounding us.

"Fireball!" he yells, gaining smiles from the people around him as he shimmies and jumps up and down.

Tessa and Luke walk hand-in-hand through the crowd toward the table we're all occupying.

The two of them disappeared immediately after the rehearsal, which Ben totally called. He said they've been looking ready to pounce on each other since they dropped the boys off in our room hours ago.

I saw some silent exchange between them while Reed and Beth were going over their vows, but in all honesty, I was too consumed in my own obsession to dissect it.

God, my husband is sexy standing barefoot in the sand. Who knew?

"Hey. Everything all right?" I ask, looking up at Tessa as Luke motions that he's headed to the bar.

"Grab me one!" Ben yells, craning his neck.

Tessa sits down beside me, her fingers drumming excitedly on her skirt. "Mm mmm," she answers.

"Mm mmm? That's it? That's all you're giving me?"

Evasive Tessa? Never met her before. She doesn't exist.

"I don't think so, missy," I murmur, leaning closer. "Spill it. You look ready to burst."

She turns her head. Her eyes glitter with contentment as they fall on Chase.

My spine straightens.

Oh, my God.

Suddenly, it all becomes clear, and my need to pry this information out of my best friend evaporates, giving way to the joy I feel in seeing her happiness.

I nudge her shoulder. "Never mind."

We exchange knowing looks as Luke returns to the table, carrying some beers for the men.

After dividing them up, Luke claims the chair next to Tessa and leans forward, elbows resting on his knees, his head turned and smiling at the little boy in my arms. He reaches out and tugs on Chase's foot, grinning even more when Chase starts kicking his legs out and giggling.

I look from Luke, to Tessa, to Ben.

His brow furrows. "Why are you crying?"

Shaking my head, I quickly wipe the tears away, mumbling about how happy I am and grimacing when my obvious emotions contradict my words.

Lord, you'd think I was pregnant already.

Ben pulls me closer against his body and kisses my temple, laughing.

A few minutes later, CJ breaks through the crowd, pointing behind him before reaching across the table for his beer.

"Hey, man. Your kid has some moves. Can you ask him to tone it down a little? He's actually stealing some of the attention away from me."

"Jealous of my boy?" Ben asks, leaning away when CJ gets a little too close for Ben's liking. "What are you doing?"

"You smell like lavender."

Ben's eyes go round. He turns, shaking his head as Tessa wails in laughter beside me.

"Taking a lot of baths, Ben?" she asks, falling against Luke and cackling.

Reed perks up, finally removing his head from Beth's neck enough to engage the rest of us in conversation.

"I thought you smelled different when we were at the rehearsal," he says, looking serious. "Not that I leaned in and inhaled or anything." He arches his brow at CJ.

"Man, whatever. I'm confident enough in my heterosexuality to notice another man's scent." He turns to Ben. "It's nice. Kind of feminine, though. If you're okay with that."

Ben exhales noisily, his arms tightening over his chest. "You said you couldn't smell it," he growls, smirking at me. "Liar."

I shrug. "You smell like Chasey. It is nice. CJ's right."

"He also said it's feminine," Luke adds, laughing. "Don't forget that. Cool for a baby. Not a grown-ass man."

Ben flips Luke off with the same hand lifting his beer. He takes a few swigs, then gestures at the crowd with his bottle.

"Hey, Reed. Isn't that your sister?"

I look up and spot Riley marching across the dance floor, pushing her way through the crowd and not looking all too pleased to be here.

She's tiny, maybe a little smaller than Tessa, with that white blonde hair her and Reed share and eyes as blue as sapphires, striking even from a distance. She's a beautiful girl, but right now she looks angry.

Angry enough to toss someone twice her size into the ocean.

Uh oh.

"Finally," Reed exclaims, sounding exhausted, shifting Beth off his lap and both of them standing.

No one seemed to know why Reed's sister skipped the rehearsal earlier. Even Beth, who is really close with Riley, appeared ignorant to the reason.

The only thing she kept saying was that Riley was dealing with stuff and would be here when she could.

I guess now is better than tomorrow, the day of the actual wedding.

"Where have you been?" Reed asks aggressively, moving closer to his sister when she reaches us. "I've been calling you for hours. You know you missed the rehearsal?"

Riley glares at Reed, then softens her gaze and sweeps it over the group, addressing all of us at once.

"Sorry I was late, but I don't really see what the big deal is. It doesn't take a genius to know how to carry a thing of flowers and walk twenty feet."

Her head tilts up as her eyes land on CJ, who is straight-up staring at her like he's possessed or something.

His body tense, yet perfectly still. Air ceasing to move in and out of his lungs.

What's his deal? And who can go this long without blinking?

Ben kicks his leg out, connecting with CJ's calf.

It startles him.

"Hey," CJ mumbles, finally snapping out of it, clearing his throat and offering his hand to Riley. "Sorry. I don't think we've met yet. I'm CJ. I'll be your partner in crime at this shindig tomorrow." He makes a weird face, looking down and murmuring, "did I really just use a cop reference?"

"Yep," Luke chuckles, leaning back and throwing his arm around Tessa. "Real smooth too."

Riley looks from Luke to CJ, then finally takes the hand

being held out for her and shakes it quickly.

"Hi," she says softly, blinking up at him. "Sorry, but I'm probably going to be a raging bitch at this thing tomorrow. Don't take it personal."

He smiles, then steps back, shoving his hands into his pockets. "Sure thing, darlin'."

"What?" Reed cuts CJ a look, then decides on addressing Riley's cryptic admission. "Why are you going to be a raging bitch? What's wrong with you?"

"You know exactly what's wrong with me. Don't play dumb, Reed."

"He's not," Ben says through a grin, attempting to lighten the mood.

It doesn't work.

He stands, looking around the group. "I'm going to take Nolan to the restroom. He's doing a different kind of dance now."

Luke gets up from his seat. "I'll join you."

I'm expecting CJ to realize how private this discussion is and step away too, even if he doesn't have to use the bathroom, but he remains where he is, keeping all of his attention fixated on Riley.

I watch Ben cross the floor and scoop up Nolan, carrying him through the crowd with Luke at his side. Once they disappear, I turn back to the drama unfolding in front of me.

I'm sticking around for moral support.

Realization dawns on Reed's face. He pulls his shoulders back. "Is this because of Dick? Are you really going to be pissed at me because I fired him? Come on, Riley. I did you a solid."

Beth tugs on Reed's arm, looking a little anxious all of a sudden.

"His name is Richard," Riley hisses. Hands clenched at

her hips. Her bottom lip trembling. "And yes, I'm going to be pissed at you for firing him. *And* for not letting him come as my date. That was a really crappy move."

Reed sighs, throwing his hands into the air. "So sorry I didn't want to pay for some ex-employee of mine to eat salmon and drink tequila shots."

"He doesn't even drink tequila! But you know who does? Me! And guess what's going on your tab, big brother?"

Riley spins on her heels, knocking into CJ before storming off in the direction of the bar.

"Whoa," Tessa murmurs.

I nod, looking from her to CJ, who grabs his beer off the table and steps away, mumbling something about needing a refill.

Reed shakes his head. "Are you kidding me? She's acting like such a child."

Beth wraps her arms around his waist from behind. "She's just upset because now things are rough between them. Give her some time. She's here. She chose sharing our day with us over sitting at home with him. That means something."

Dropping his head, looking half ready to pass out and half ready to sweep Beth into his arms and pin her against something, Reed turns and gathers his soon-to-be wife against his chest, pressing his mouth to her hair and whispering.

After a moment, he looks over at the two of us. "We're going to go take a walk on the beach."

"Cool. We'll probably turn in soon," Tessa replies, both of us waving when Beth raises her hand.

"That was crazy," I murmur, shifting Chase in my arms after they move away. "And did you see CJ staring at Riley? I thought he was going to grab her by the hair and drag her off to his villa for a quick bang. Is he out of his mind? Reed will kill him."

"Weddings," Tessa snickers, turning her head and smiling at me. "Tomorrow should be interesting."

Nodding, I lean against her, the two of us falling into a fit of quiet giggles and no doubt picturing the same scenario in our minds, involving Reed tackling one of his groomsmen to the ground while his sister pummels him in the back with her bouquet.

Thank God we brought headphones for Nolan's iPad. He might just be wearing those during the ceremony.

After Ben and Luke return to the table with Nolan, we all order some food and hang out a bit longer, laughing as Luke recalls some of the things Nolan was trying to pull over on him while staying at their house.

Telling Luke he was allowed to buy whatever apps he wanted because he's such a good kid. Flipping through On Demand and acting like he watches Game of Thrones regularly.

By the time our meals are finished, Chase is asleep in Ben's arms and Nolan is showing the first signs of being tired, little yawns he tries to conceal because he wants to stay up and dance some more.

Tessa and Luke head for the bar, not ready to call it a night yet. Ben takes Chase back to the room while I let Nolan hear one final song.

The last note plays. My little dancer looks ready to drop.

I scoop Nolan up into my arms and carry him through the small crowd, his body immediately going limp with exhaustion and melting against mine.

God, I love this little boy.

I press gentle kisses to his cheek, smelling the sand and saltwater on his skin. When I'm almost at our villa, I reach into my back pocket, carefully balancing Nolan in one arm so I can pull out my keycard and not disturb him.

I step up to the door. The sound of one closing behind me draws my attention over my shoulder.

Riley emerges from the villa beside ours, the ivory strapless dress she's wearing looking a little more wrinkled than it should. Her hair tangled, half coming out of the jeweled clip she was securing it up with, and feet bare. Her sandals tucked under her arm.

She looks like someone who's just had wild, uninhibited sex.

That's odd. Why would she look like someone who's just had wild, uninhibited sex? Isn't her boyfriend at home?

I look at the side of the villa, then at her again, and it dawns on me, exactly who is sleeping in that villa this weekend.

Not Reed and Beth. Not Luke and Tessa. And definitely not Riley.

My eyes widen.

Oh, shit.

Riley lifts her head with a gasp, finally noticing me standing here, her eyes doubling in size and somehow looking more startled than mine.

I stare at her. She stares at me.

An exchange happens between us, a silent plea from her mouth to my ears.

Don't tell Reed. Please, Mia.

With a frantic shake of her head, Riley turns and hurries down the footpath, disappearing around the bend.

"Hey."

I yelp, startled by the deep voice behind me, my hands squeezing Nolan a little tighter as he stirs in my arms.

Spinning around, I gather my breath and smile shakily at Reed. "God, you scared me."

"I can see that."

He glances over my shoulder, then draws his eyes back to my face.

I relax when I don't notice any suspicion in his stare.

Wow. What incredible timing. Five seconds earlier and Riley would've been totally busted.

"Have you seen Riley?"

FUCK.

I blink at him. "Um, who?"

Reed breathes a laugh, giving me an odd look. "Riley. My sister. Angry blonde who is out to kill me." He rakes a hand through his hair and looks out over the beach. "I wanted to apologize but she's not in her room. Think she might still be at the bar?"

I nod when he turns back to me. "Absolutely. Yep. I'm certain that's where she is. Why would she be over here? That's just crazy."

Again, Reed cocks his head, his eyebrow lifting in curiosity.

Oh, my God, Mia. You would make a terrible spy. Stop talking.

"Yeah, all right." Reed nods. He looks convinced. "I'm going to go look for her. I'll see you tomorrow."

"Okay."

He walks down the path in the direction of the bar.

I collapse against the door the second Reed disappears from my sight.

My pulse is racing, fluttering like hummingbird wings beneath my ear. My skin feels a little clammy.

I hate secrets. And I am not taking on this burden alone. No, thank you. If I'm going to freak out, someone else is going to freak out right along with me.

Unlocking the door, I push into the room and spot Ben on the bed.

"CJ and Riley just had sex. Wild, all over the room kind of sex. I'm sure of it."

Ben glances up briefly from the T.V., then resumes watching. His shoulder jerks. "I could've called that."

His tone is cavalier. Completely unaffected.

It baffles me. *Does he not know how this will end?*

I carry Nolan over to the bed and lay him down next to Chase, tucking him under the covers. Moving around to the other side, I straddle Ben's lap and block his view of whatever show is captivating him more than this unbelievable drama.

"Do you know what's going to happen when Reed finds out?"

"Who said Reed has to find out?"

I gape at him. "If they start dating, you don't think it'll be obvious?"

Ben snorts, pulling my waist and drawing me closer. "Maybe they just wanted to fuck. People do that, Mia. It ain't always about being in a relationship with someone."

I arch my brow.

He hovers his mouth over mine. "Unless it's you and me."

"Good save," I whisper, leaning in and kissing him slowly, forgetting about anything outside of this room and once again being all-consumed by this man. "I want to do more than this, but I think we better let the boys sleep."

His hands roam down my back to my ass, squeezing me there. "Yeah," he murmurs.

"You going to be okay with just a kiss right now?"

His breathing pauses.

Leaning back, Ben takes my face between his hands and runs his thumb over my lip, smearing the moisture there and staring at my mouth.

"Yeah. That's one helluva kiss, Georgia."

I blink, my own breath catching somewhere in my throat as I remember that night at the bar and those words and Ben, his beautiful face squinting across the parking lot, gaze narrowing in on my old license plate before he took me home and I never left.

He didn't know who I was. I didn't think I knew him. But we were wrong.

And it was perfect.

Tugging him off the bed, my heart pounding now for an entirely different reason, I slowly back across the room with his hand in mine.

"I think it's time for another bath," I whisper, wiggling my brows.

Ben laughs. I squeal, jumping into his arms the second he strips off his shirt.

"No bubbles."

I smile against his mouth. "I love you."

"That's all I need, baby," he says, positioning himself to take me. "All I'll ever fucking need."

I close my eyes, feeling him stretch me. Fill me.

And I'm home.

The End

Read on for a bonus scene from

luke & tessa

luke & tessa

I DON'T KNOW how the fuck anyone with kids gets any sleep at night.

Leaning against my old bedroom wall, my arms folded tightly across my chest and my breathing anxious as shit, I stare across the room, shifting my restless gaze between the twin bed—my old bed growing up, and the portable crib set up by the window. The two small bodies occupying them keeping me on edge like nothing else I've ever felt.

Keeping me here, right the fuck here, in this room.

Stressed as a motherfucker.

Tessa and I put Nolan and Chase to bed over two hours ago. That went down a lot easier than I was anticipating.

A lot fucking easier. Especially after seeing how damn excited Nolan was about staying at my place for the next two days while Ben and Mia get some time alone.

The kid went a little psycho about it. Filming himself in every room with his iPad. Taking a fuck-ton of selfies with me.

And I don't do selfies, but it's Nolan, so fuck it, I did selfies.

A lot of fucking selfies.

He even insisted on him and Chase getting their heights measured out on the wall in my kitchen below mine and Tessa's.

"We're gonna live here too, Uncle Luke," he told me, smiling proudly at his mark while running his finger across it.

"We'll have two houses. This one, and Daddy's. We can stay here on the weekends and do cool stuff with you."

I couldn't help but grin.

Cool stuff with me, 'cause I'm a pretty cool motherfucker to a six-year-old, taking selfies every five seconds or sooner, if he insists.

And he insisted.

Keeping the boys outside most of the night, running around and chasing after Max tired them out quick. Chase couldn't keep his eyes open by seven-thirty. Nolan could barely walk up the stairs, and neither one of them put up a fight when we guided them into my old room and told them it was time to go to sleep.

Chase dozed off first. Almost instantly, courtesy of the noise his big brother was making. After covering the little man up, I took my guitar from Nolan and he climbed up into bed, clutching that dragon he's had since he was a baby.

His eyes closed within seconds.

The house went still.

And Tessa? She passed out cold in our bed the second she stretched out beneath the sheets.

Normally I'd be in there with her, keeping her flush against me, cock to ass, my hand cupping her tit as I debated fucking or sleeping, fucking normally winning out every damn time and her, being Tessa, going with it and giving as good as she got, but instead I'm in here, watching over my nephews like I'm damn-near terrified they'll stop breathing or something.

I've checked to make sure that hasn't happened at least five times now, hand close to their face or on their chest, feeling the expansion of their lungs and, seconds later, the relieved compression of mine.

Stressful. As. Fuck.

How do parents do it? How do they put their kids to bed at night and get a fucking minute of sleep themselves?

I guess this comes with the territory. Being a dad means putting yourself last, your kids and woman first, making sure they get everything they need; roof over their heads, hot meals and beds to sleep in at night, and also, case in point right fucking now, guaranteeing they are living those lives you're willing to die to give them, and doing it peacefully under that roof you provided.

Not losing consciousness in the middle of the night because you weren't fucking paying attention to what mattered most, because you were a selfish prick who thought about getting a minute of shut-eye yourself.

Fuck that.

If this is what it takes, if this is what comes with getting a family of your own, having the woman you love give you that family and trusting you to take care of it, relying on you to be her man and a father and not a selfish prick who cares more about himself than what really fucking matters, I'm down with it.

I'm down with all of it.

A quiet grunt lifts my head. Arms still tight across my chest, my eyes narrow in the darkness, spotting the crib by the window.

Chase.

Motherfucker.

I shove off the wall and stalk across the room, stopping beside the crib and bending down to examine the little man sleeping.

He is on his back, just like he was five minutes ago when I last stalked over here, body limp except for the arm he has wrapped tight around his stuffed octopus. That damn thing shoved in his face, right against his mouth and nose, obstructing his breathing. A-fuckin'-gain.

Smothering him.

Probably restricting his oxygen and slowly taking his life.

I've moved that motherfucker away from his mouth three times now. Three fucking times. What the fuck? He can't just stay asleep and leave it where I put it, which is way the hell away from his face.

This is the main reason why I'm not asleep, my mind at ease and my hand squeezing one of Tessa's perfect tits. I gotta make sure Chase doesn't kill himself with this bastard stuffed animal I'm two seconds away from throwing outside or feeding to Max.

Reaching down, again, I grab a tentacle and pull the octopus to the edge of the crib.

Chase groans. His eyes flutter.

With a fucking sneer I know he's directing at me, even though the room is near pitch black and he seems to be completely out of it and not focusing on anything in particular, and like I'm not saving his precious little life right now, he grabs that same damn tentacle, flips over onto his stomach, and pins the octopus to the crib with his arm, his face smashed right up against it.

Right. The fuck. Up against it.

Mouth and nose.

"Goddamn it, little man. You're really starting to piss me off."

"What are you doing?"

I lift my head and turn it, spotting Tessa in the doorway.

Head cocked to the side, hair all messy and wild from sleep, big and looking like I've had my hands in it, which immediately starts doing things to my dick, the knuckles of one hand digging into her right eye, the other eye pinning me with confusion.

I straighten and brace my hands on the edge of the crib, shifting slightly to face her.

"Saving Chase from a slow, painful death. One he keeps insisting on meeting tonight while he's in our care, which I really don't fucking appreciate."

She straightens too, pushing off from the frame, looking even more confused as she pads slowly across the room, her curious eyes slicing between me and the crib.

"He's trying to kill himself?" she asks, stopping beside me and gazing down at Chase, the end of her question breaking with a yawn.

"Yeah."

"And how's he trying to do that?"

I gesture at the obvious scene in front of me.

"You serious? Look how he's got that piece of shit right up against his face. He can't breathe like that. I know he can't breathe like that. I've been standing in this room listening to him make these scary-as-fuck suffocating noises in the back of his throat for the past forty-five minutes, startling himself enough to partially wake, resituate himself, where, like a pain in my ass, he decides to stupidly put that piece of shit bastard stuffed animal up against his face again and pass back out, only to cut off his air supply five fucking minutes later. I keep taking it away from him and moving it out of reach, not out of the crib 'cause I know he'll really freak if I do that and I don't want to wake Nolan, but just out of the way of his face, and you know what he does? He fucking shoots me this look like I'm getting on his fucking nerves, not saving his life, grabs that piece of shit, rolls over or whatever he needs to do to get more comfortable, and proceeds to press his face in it again while he dozes back off."

Tessa laughs softly.

I wrap my hands around the edge of the crib again, tightening my grip as I look between her and Chase.

"Now you see what I mean when I say he's trying to kill himself? The kid has a death wish, and honest to fucking God, he's giving me chest pains."

Tessa stares up at me, eyes round and no longer holding a shred of sleepiness to them, her mouth slowly curving up in one corner, then the other, her cheeks lifting, and proceeds to then break into a quiet, yet still fully amused and solely at my expense laugh, dropping her head until it hits my arm with a soft thud.

"Oh, my God," she whispers, her shoulders shaking. "You look ready to kill Chase. Straight up."

Kill him?

"I'm saving his life."

"You're pissed off," another cackle then, "'cause Chase is giving you dirty looks."

I watch her hand come up and cover her mouth, quieting her laughter.

"Poor kid only wants to sleep with the stuffed animal he's slept with his entire life, Luke. The same one he's never suffocated from. Never came close to suffocating from. And you're the big meanie taking it from him."

"Fucking miracle he hasn't suffocated," I cut back, glaring at the octopus, then whipping my head around and aiming that glare at the top of Tessa's head. "A big meanie? I'm mean for keeping him alive?"

She turns fully to me at the same time as I turn fully to her, her hands forming to my waist where she squeezes with each gasp of breath she takes between giggles, her body jolting against mine.

"I'm not seeing anything funny about this," I growl, tilting my head down when she lifts hers, the look I'm giving her conveying my feelings and ceasing her laughter.

"The kid is seriously stressing me out."

Tessa pulls her lips tight, fighting that smile, her hands still clutching at my sides.

"I can see that."

"Seriously stressing me out," I reaffirm.

Another lip twitch, which she conceals quickly.

"How dare he."

"But I want this."

That gets her.

Mouth instantly going slack, eyes no longer creasing in the corners and instead going round the way they do when I say important shit to her, maybe even going a little bigger this time from these words, words I need to get out and, more importantly, I need her to fucking hear, her hands relaxing to my hips where I barely feel them anymore.

"Want . . . what?" she whispers, staring up at me.

"This," I reply, tipping my chin at the crib and the bed against the wall, moving a little closer and securing my arms around her waist so she can't run away from this or me, knowing damn well that's what she wants to do right now and preventing it.

She's been avoiding this conversation for months. I'm tired of her avoiding it.

Tessa goes still. Her lips part with a gasp.

I continue with a squeeze of my hands, keeping my voice low, but steady and sure.

"Want this with you. I want to be standing here going out of my fucking mind 'cause our kid is shoving some motherfucking toy against his face and making noises that scare the shit outta me. I want that same kid, or another one you give me, forcing me to take selfies every five seconds in every goddamn room of this house, marking their growth on that wall in our kitchen and looking at it every time I go in there, loving that it's there and, if we happen to want or need a bigger place because you keep giving me kids, which, babe, you want my dick, you know you got it. Ten, twenty kids, I don't care. You give them to me, I'll want them, cutting that same piece of wood from the wall in our kitchen and taking it with us, 'cause it sure as shit ain't getting left behind."

Tessa blinks, opens her mouth to try and talk her way out of this conversation, 'cause she's my woman and that's what she does when something's too heavy for her to take on and she can't escape, attempts to speak, then clamps her mouth shut again when I cut her off and keep going.

"I want this, babe," I tell her, angling my head to get closer, my hands moving up her back to her shoulders and neck, to the sides of her face where I hold her there. "I want this more than I can remember wantin' anything, aside from wantin' you, and I wanted that a whole fuckin' lot, Tessa."

Her lips quivers.

"Still do. Nothing changing that. Nothing could change it, and I think you know I'm being serious right now, considering what all we went through. And speaking of that, babe," I pause, breathing in her gasp when I put my mouth an inch from hers. "What happened in the past with us, is in the past. I can't change it. You can't change it. You thought you were carrying my kid. You knew I didn't want it, which, telling you right the fuck now, I would've wanted it, considering you were part of that package and I'll always want whatever I can get that gives me you. Know that. The shit that happened back then and the shit that followed, got us to here. Got me to seeing my girl wearing my ring and looking so damn happy every time I see her looking at it, hearing the excitement in her voice when she introduces me as her man, and seeing my name attached to hers, knowing it'll always be attached to hers. Always, babe. I can't regret any of that. Not when I'm standing here with you right now. Not when I get to live the rest of my life knowing I have you, and further knowing what all I want out of the rest of my life, which includes starting a family with the only woman I care to give my ring to, attach my name to, and hear introducing me as her man."

"Luke," Tessa whispers, her pink lip still quivering.

"I'm not done," I inform her.

She blinks, then nods her head still encased by my hands. "Okay."

I keep on.

"I know you're scared. I know the shit we've been through gives you that right to be scared, but I'm telling you, Tessa, on my fucking life, I will never put you through that kind of pain again. I'll fuck up, no doubt piss you off occasionally, maybe frequently, but I know you fucking thrive on that shit and get off on it so I'm not too worried about arguments or fights over who the fuck is going to do the dishes or why my dirty clothes are on the floor, which, babe, just so you know, I get off on it too so please keep running your mouth about how you're sick of my shit, 'cause I fucking love it, but what I am saying is I ain't leaving. I will never leave you again. I gave you that ring, my last name, and my fucking life. A life I want filled with you and the family we'll share together. I want that. This." I shift my eyes to the crib and bed, then back to Tessa. "But only if I can have it with you."

We stare at each other for what feels like a lifetime. My

heart beating so loudly I can hear it in my ears.

Tessa tips her head up, suddenly looking defiant.

Shit.

"I do not get off on you leaving your dirty clothes on the floor," she snaps, rolling up on her toes to get closer. "Nothing hot about that, Luke."

My back goes straight. My hands dropping to my sides.

"Babe, seriously? That's what you got outta what I just said?"

Unfuckingbelievable.

"No," she quickly replies. "That's not what I got outta what you just said, but it's part of it. I also heard you telling me you only want it to be me wearing your ring and claiming your last name, for-fucking-ever, you like me telling people you're my man, which, just so you know, I fucking love saying it so even if you didn't like hearing it, I'd still say it. Not needing your permission, *babe*."

I shake my head.

Jesus Christ.

She keeps right on going, bringing her hand to her hip.

"Also heard you saying you like fighting with me, which is why I'm running my mouth right now instead of getting all emotional on you after you just said the most beautiful words to me I have ever heard in . . . my . . . life, more beautiful than what you said the day we got married, and," she cocks her head, "honest to God, Luke, didn't think you could top that day, but you just did. So, I'm giving you my mouth the way you like it 'cause I know you get off on that and there are several choice places I'd like your mouth to be right now, and I'd appreciate it finding it's way to those choice places sooner rather than later after taking in everything you just said, which, babe, was the most I've ever heard you say in a conversation. Like, ever."

I stare down at her, feeling a few of her words hit me straight in my dick.

Several choice places I'd like your mouth to be.

Fuck yeah.

I move in, ready to pounce on my woman but Tessa thwarts my advances with a firm hand to my chest.

Something moves over her face as I lean back. Her eyes gentle. She swallows thickly, then proceeds to give me the tiniest voice I've ever heard her use.

"You want this? Like, really *really* want it?"

"Babe." I tilt my head. "Yeah. What did I just say?"

"And you're sure . . . I mean, you're positive you want this with me?"

"Tess . . ." I start, but she jumps back in, fisting my shirt as she continues.

"Forever, Luke. I'm talking about you being tied to me forever. 'Cause even if this somehow didn't work out . . ."

"It will," I assure her.

"But even if it didn't . . ."

I grab her arms firmly.

"It will, babe. I'm not going anywhere. Not without you."

She scrapes her teeth across her bottom lip, dropping her eyes to my shirt.

"You'll be stuck with me," she murmurs. "Stuck for life like Ben is stuck with Angie. That situation isn't so bad now, but still, something happens to us and you move on, you find someone like Ben found Mia, I don't think I could . . ."

I've had about enough of this bullshit.

Tugging her, I press her against me, pinning us chest to chest, or, more accurately because of the height difference, tits to stomach, my arms snaking around her back and tightening, ignoring the cute little gasp she gives me and taking over this conversation before she says something else to piss me off.

"Without you for a year," I growl, seeing the memory I'm pulling from hit her like a jolt of lightening, her spine going stiff and her eyes instantly filling with tears.

"Luke," she whispers.

"A year, Tessa," I continue. "Never moved on. I thought about you every day. Thought about how I fucked up and driving myself crazy thinking about it, trying to stay pissed at you for not telling me about the kid, which only made me think about you even more, knowing I had to stop thinking about you and move the fuck on, but couldn't. Never . . . hear me, babe, I never had that with a girl. Never thought about someone the way I thought about you, and babe, the way I thought about you I knew even then that shit was sticking with me for life."

She blinks, sending tears halfway down her cheek before I swipe them away with my thumbs.

"I wanted to be tied to you since you hopped outta your brother's truck, walked your sexy ass over to me and refused to shake my hand, giving me that smile that's both sweet as hell and has the ability to make me think about doing other things to your mouth, besides watching you use it in sweet ways. You askin' me if I want this, I'm telling you," I lean in closer. "I want it. I want it today. I'll want it a fucking year from now. I'll want it when I'm too old to tell you I want it, so yeah, babe. I'm sure. Never been more sure about anything, except the day I saw you, hopping outta your brother's truck."

"Oh, my God," she says breathlessly.

"I see you're getting me now."

About fucking time.

That soft, on-the-verge-of-more-tears face vanishes before

me. Her expression tightens up, and with quick hands she shoves hard against my chest, sending me a couple inches backwards since she catches me off guard.

"The fuck, Tessa?"

I mean to say more. I mean to ask her why she pushed me and to possibly prepare myself to inform her, again, my clear as fuckin' day, in my opinion, views on this topic but she hurls herself into my arms and shuts me up with the kiss to beat all fuckin' kisses.

Wet and sweet. Rough and crazed.

Just like my woman.

"You are such an asshole," she says while hitching her legs around my waist, her hands digging into my shoulders and sliding to the back of my scalp where she drags her nails, sending a chill up my spine.

So good.

"You know I can't handle sweet from you. That isn't *you*, Luke. I know you, and I get off on you, then you throw sweet at me and I'm unprepared for that and it does weird shit to me like almost bring me to orgasm just from your sweet and what the fuck?"

Her last three words are pressed against my jaw where she bites and licks my skin, then moves back to my mouth, giving me her tongue, hot and wild.

Christ. She's mad and horny.

Fucking love that.

I get us out into the hallway before I rip her clothes off and take her right there next to Chase's crib.

"What? It's the truth," I tell her, kicking our bedroom door open and tossing her onto the bed.

She sits up, pulling her shirt over her head and ridding herself of her panties, her eyes on me while I toss my own shirt and make quick work of my belt.

"Too sweet." She shakes her head. "I'm pretty sure the second your tongue hits my clit, I'm coming."

"Wouldn't be the first time."

Her eyes narrow as she watches me crawl toward her after stepping out of my pants and boxers, her head hitting the pillow and her knees dropping to the side, allowing me to push my shoulders between them and whisper against her cunt.

"Ask me."

She moans, fingers digging at my scalp as I lick where she's wettest, dragging my tongue over her clit until her legs shake.

She wasn't lying. Her first orgasm hits seconds into it, thighs clamping against my ears and nails breaking the skin of my shoulders.

"Shit." She arches off the bed. "Oh, God, Luke . . . fuck."

I keep at her, eating her roughly, moaning when she grates her heels into my back and fucking her with my tongue when she lifts her hips, pressing unashamedly against my face.

"Waiting, babe," I say after releasing her clit from between my teeth.

I lift my head, meeting her eyes glazed over with need and want, her tongue darting out, chest heaving with sharp breaths, showing me that fire she has every time I'm building her.

She lifts her legs higher, spreading more for me and tugging at my arms to ease me up her body.

"Do you . . . Luke!"

I flip her on her stomach before she has a chance to get out her question and pull back, her slim hips in my hands, bringing her to her knees, the tip of my cock rubbing between her ass until she drops down . . .

Lower.

Lower.

Her cheek pressing to the mattress, her ass high in the air, pushing back as an offering to me which I waste no time in taking.

Grunting, I slide home, yanking her back, fingers digging into flesh until I'm fully inside.

She stretches her arms above her head and claws at the sheets.

"Damn," I growl.

I watch my cock move in and out, keeping my pace and slowly building us.

"You want it?"

Tessa turns her head and nods, her lips parted with a moan.

She thinks I'm talking about her taking my cock. I know she wants that. Fucking sure of it. No need to confirm.

"Want it with me?" I ask, getting to my point and not stopping there, even when I see my meaning dawn on her face, but driving it home and making it stick while I fuck her.

"Being serious, babe. You say you want it, want everything I'm fuckin' sure of and have been sure of for a long fuckin' time, I'm looking at getting you knocked up tonight. No joke. You ain't starting that new pack of birth control that's sitting on the counter. That shit is going straight in the garbage. By me. I'm going to fuck you. Take a break. Fuck you again. Check on the boys, 'cause you know Chase is acting suicidal in there, then come back in here and let you ride me so I can watch your tits."

I slide my hand around her waist and dip it between her legs.

She gasps, writhing against me and pumping back to get me going faster.

I give her faster.

Harder.

Watching her hands curl into fists on the sheet.

"Yes," she pants, giving me her answer as I move my thumb over her clit.

"You want it?"

"Yes."

"Want it with me?"

"YES," she moans, head dropping. "God, Luke . . . oh, fuck. F-Fuck."

Her pussy clenches around my dick.

Hard.

She wants it with me.

Wants a family, kids, all of it . . . with me.

Couldn't hold off coming now if I tried.

I wrap my arm around her chest, my other around her waist and pull, bringing her up as I pump my hips and go off deep inside her cunt, her hands reaching back and sliding over my thighs to my ass, pulling me even deeper as she turns her head and claims my mouth in a long, hard kiss.

Wet and sweet. Rough and crazed.

"Forever, babe," I tell her, kissing her gently, pushing her sweaty hair out of her eyes, my cock still buried deep and her arms still clutching at me.

"For-fucking-ever," I whisper.

She smiles against my mouth before leaning forward to untangle us, then turning and wrapping her arms around my neck, giving me a hard squeeze.

Her tongue tastes my bottom lip.

"Heads up. There's a real good chance I'll be a raging bitch when I'm pregnant and you'll be getting the brunt of my mood swings and probable violent tendencies, more than probable death threats for putting me in that situation in the first place. You might be regretting all this forever talk."

It's my turn to smile, and I do it pushing my hand into her hair and tilting her, angling to get more of that mouth I'm completely fucking gone for.

"Countin' on it, babe. You know I get off on that."

She shakes her head through a laugh, touching her forehead to mine before giving me that kiss.

And I fucking take it.

All of it.

For-fucking-ever.

acknowledgements

I'M GOING TO keep this thank you simple.

Thank you to every reader who fell in love with Ben and the rest of my Bama Boys. Your enthusiasm for their stories inspires me every day.

books by
J. DANIELS

SWEET ADDICTION SERIES
Sweet Addiction
Sweet Possession
Sweet Obsession
Sweet Love (Coming Soon)

ALABAMA SUMMER SERIES
Where I Belong
All I Want
When I Fall
Where We Belong
What I Need
So Much More (Halloween Novella)
All We Want
Say I'm Yours (Coming Soon)

DIRTY DEEDS SERIES
Four Letter Word
Hit the Spot
Bad for You
Down too Deep (Coming Soon)

about the author

J DANIELS IS THE *New York Times* and *USA Today* bestselling author of the Sweet Addiction series, the Alabama Summer series, and the Dirty Deeds series.

She would rather bake than cook, she listens to music entirely too loud, and loves writing stories her children will never read. Her husband and children are her greatest loves, with cupcakes coming in at a close second.

J grew up in Baltimore and resides in Maryland with her family.

follow ʝ at:

www.authorjdaniels.com

Facebook
www.facebook.com/jdanielsauthor

Twitter—@JDanielsbooks

Instagram—authorjdaniels

Goodreads
http://bit.ly/JDanielsGoodreads

Join her reader's group for the first look at upcoming projects, special giveaways, and loads of fun!
www.facebook.com/groups/JsSweeties

Sign up to receive her newsletter and get special offers and exclusive release info.
www.authorjdaniels.com/newsletter

playlist

Ride by Chase Rice
Put that shit on repeat.

Made in United States
Orlando, FL
05 January 2023